J.T. DOSSETT

Armandus' Absolution

outskirtspress
DENVER, COLORADO

Outskirts Press, Inc.
http://www.outskirtspress.com

ISBN: 978-1-4787-5723-8

Outskirts Press and the "OP" logo are trademarks belonging to Outskirts Press, Inc.

"The weak can never forgive. Forgiveness is the
attribute of the strong."
— *Mahatma Gandhi*

To Brenda

NOVELS BY J.T. DOSSETT

Finding Bobby Ray
Glory on Stinking Creek
Starvin' Dog and the Guardians

CONTENTS

FOREWORD

Thank God for search engines. It's a blessing to have information literally at your fingertips, especially when you are writing a book. I remember when research was drudgery—going to the library, struggling with the Dewey Decimal System, waiting to discover the answers to my questions before I could continue with my work. This book is comprised of a lot of historical information; however, I have massaged some of it to fit within the timeline of my story. The story covers a period of over twenty years, spanning geography from Belgium to East Tennessee to Africa; there are foreign expressions, names of towns, medical terminology that I have gleaned with the help of information contained from search engines—stuff in the public domain. I have taken poetic license from some facts and matters to create an effect. The grist for this book is based upon the impact of forgiveness and its karmic attributes, forgiveness as it pertains to the quality of your life and to the quality of others' lives. Please understand that I am not professing to be an expert on forgiveness; I'm not very good at it, but I am learning, and I've learned more from writing this novel. My hope is that you will forgive me for my transgressions. And to all of you, please realize my sincerity when I say, *Tu es pardonné.*
JTD
Campbell County
March 15, 2015

BOOK 1
WAR IN THE FOREST

Chapter 1

THE ARDENNES

The Germans called it *"Unternehmen Wacht an Rhein"*—The Watch on the Rhine. The French called it *"Bataille des Ardennes"*—Battle of the Ardennes. It became the bloodiest battle fought in the Great War, as America and its allies struggled to repress the offensive of the German Army to recapture the significant harbor of Antwerp, Belgium. Hitler's plan was to rip a hole in the British and American line, and with this turgid effort, ultimately destroy four allied armies. Initially, the Americans labeled the clash "The Ardennes Counter Offensive." However, because the Allied Front Line appeared to bulge inward on war maps, the conflict was labeled by the media as "the Battle of the Bulge." The Allied campaign was also known as *Hell* to some members of the Tennessee 117th Infantry Regiment and their comrades of the 30th Infantry Division.

It stopped snowing, finally, and warmed up a bit, much to the relief of the patrol. They had spent the last three weeks trudging through knee-deep snow in the tracks, choking on the exhaust fumes of the M4 Sherman tanks as they moved onward through the Ardennes Forest toward their destination: St. Vith. The village was a French-speaking community in the Belgian province of Leige. The Germans had attempted to use this undulating, forested region twice as an invasion course into Northern France and Southern Belgium, and failed. But the area remained saturated with German troops eager to regain control of the town, even after the 30th Infantry Division, with the help of heavy air support, had driven them out, inflicting heavy casualties.

Sergeant Bowman Rafferty and members of his squad hunkered at the edge of the forest, peering at the farmhouse in the distance. Command had sent them from St. Vith to ferret out pockets of the enemy, who were taking sly advantage of the cover provided by the nearly impenetrable wooded Ardennes region of Wallonia.

It was dark on the perimeter of the foreboding forest. But in the clear, which wasn't very clear, the winter sky reluctantly shed its yellow-gray light, which was further diffused by the soupy fog that rose from the fields to absorb it.

As Rafferty scanned the sepia-toned, gauzily veiled clearing, he was having difficulty defining objects in the distance, even with the use of field glasses.

"My grandfather had a farm that looked just like this in upper New York State. We spent a lot of good summers there," said Corporal Milord.

"I'll bet you didn't have Krauts for playmates," whispered Rafferty, and he stiffened as the orange glow from a light melted through the murk.

"Light just came on in the house; there's some movement; probably eating breakfast," said Rafferty, who, despite the prodding razor tip of danger and depressing dreariness, remembered fondly mornings on his father's farm in East Tennessee; the terrain there was quite similar to this area, but certainly, not as cold; certainly, not as hostile.

"So, what do you have on your list of things to do today, Armandus?" said his mother, Adelheide, as she poured milk on his bowl of muesli.

"I'm going to hitch the Heavy Horses to the sled and go to the woods to hunt for firewood," said the boy as he crunched a mouthful of rolled oats, seeds, dried fruit, and nuts.

The stout, rosy-cheeked woman nodded her head satisfactorily as she placed buttered bread and sliced Gouda cheese before him. It didn't seem like a sufficient breakfast to fuel the boy through an entire day of hard work, but it was more than many had in these trying times. Before he was killed, Adelheide's husband, Sander, had anticipated hardships brought on by the war, and provided a well-stocked larder in the pantry and in the springhouse to sustain his family through the winter and beyond. As fate would have it, he was in the town of St. Vith, scavenging what meager supplies were available, when RAF Lancaster bombers destroyed most of the town, sending the Germans packing from where they were ensconced. Sander was killed when a wall of a building caved in on him. Devastated at the loss of husband and father, Armandus and Adelheide continued their dismal lives, shocked and confounded.

Adelheide reached in her apron pocket and produced an envelope.

"Look what I received in town yesterday!" she said, smiling.

"Is it from Christophe?" he replied excitedly, reaching for the letter which she deftly snatched away from his grasp.

She squinted at the postmark.

"Yes, who else? But it is postmarked at least a month ago. That was before he left school in Antwerp for his job," she said, and Armandus knew that Christophe's "job" had something to do with the resistance movement against the German occupation.

"We will read it tonight at supper. It will make for a nice evening," said Adelheide, tucking the letter back into her apron pocket, and placing two apples and a small bunch of carrots on the table in front of Armandus.

"Here are treats for the Brabançon—draft horses need to eat too."

"They will love these treats, especially the apples, even though they are soft. I went to the barn earlier and fed them their oats," he said, stuffing the fruit and vegetables into the pockets of his drab wool coat as he rose from the table. He hugged his mother as she tied a scarf around his neck, buttoned his coat, and snugged a woolen cap on his head, as if he were a five-year-old trekking out to build a snowman. She set a large brown bag with the edges tightly rolled on the tabletop.

"I've packed you a good lunch: a sausage sandwich with sauce andalouse, some Gouda cheese, and a pint of Genever; you might want to share that with the horses too; wait a minute," she said as she rushed from the kitchen. She returned with the shotgun. "You take this with you; here are some extra shells; you never know when you might need it," she warned nervously.

"Thank you, Mamma. I'll be careful," he said, expertly loading the weapon.

"I love you, Son. You and Christophe are my life. Hurry home, we are having chicken waterzooi for supper this evening."

He clapped his hands together, making a soft popping sound with his woolen mittens.

"I'll be home early—with a load of firewood to warm you, Mamma!" he said as he took lively steps out the door into the fog.

The horses, beautifully matched chestnuts, seventeen hands high and weighing about two thousand pounds each, munched contentedly on the carrots and apples as Armandus hitched the animals to the sleigh. He was about to load up the crosscut saw, some rope, and an axe when he heard a scratching noise carried on the fog from the springhouse, which was located on the creek at the edge of the forest.

"Damned fox. Trying to burrow under the springhouse again," he muttered, grabbing the shotgun, striding toward the noise.

"Whoa! We've got movement in the barnyard," said Rafferty, passing the glasses to Milord.

"Looks like the uniform of some enlisted swine, not very fancy, but worth taking down," said Milord, shouldering his carbine, attempting to draw a bead on the figure that drifted like a wraith through the blanket of fog.

"Hold on. Let's make sure what we're shooting at, if we shoot at all," said Rafferty, who was peering through the field glasses again at the figure that was walking swiftly to the cover of the springhouse. "Looks like he's carrying a weapon," said Rafferty, shouldering his M1A1 carbine and adjusting the sights. He could knock a squirrel out of a tree at twenty yards back home with his .22, and he was proficient as anyone with this rifle.

"How many yards do you think the target is away, Milord?"

"Has to be about 175 yards, Sarge."

"We'll wait. This piece of shit is inaccurate at 150 yards," he replied, squinting through the sight.

Armandus stopped short of the springhouse, smiling as the ravenous fox, oblivious to his presence, worked diligently to dig beneath the building. The boy, blessed with a tender heart, felt sorry for the emaciated animal.

"I would sooner open the door for you, Reynard, but Mamma and I have to eat this winter too," he said, removing the safety on the shotgun. "Instead, I will save your life. Run, little red man," Armandus said as he fired the weapon in the air.

Adelheide shook her head and clucked when she noticed that Armandus had forgotten his lunch.

"That boy is so forgetful," she said as she reached for her coat, which was hanging on the hook by the door. She flinched when she heard the report of the shotgun and the crack of a rifle from a distance.

The fox flew in the direction of the woods, but briefly changed course as a shot was fired from where he was destined. Mortally wounded in the neck, Armandus ran a few steps and fell heavily into a snow bank, where it quickly turned cherry red from the spillage. The horses were whinnying nervously from the barn as Adelheide screamed in agony from the porch.

Rafferty was able to issue orders, although he was shaken, aware that he'd made a ghastly mistake.

"You men cover the barn; you men, search the outbuildings; you men, go to that woman on the porch," he ordered as he and Milord crept cautiously toward the prostrate form in the darkening snow.

"Goddammit!" said Rafferty as he rolled the dying boy on his back.

"It's okay, Sarge, I thought he was a Kraut too," said Milord shakily.

"Somebody get a medic over here," Rafferty screamed hoarsely, as he attempted to stanch the gushing blood with his hands.

The boy moaned, and grabbed Rafferty's hand with his own. He whispered something in French. "Milord, you speak a little French, what did he say?" cried Rafferty, leaning close to the boy's bloodied face.

"He said 'I am dying,'" said Milord, holding his hand over his own eyes, unable to look at Armandus or Rafferty.

Rafferty sighed heavily, holding the boy's head tightly in his arms.

"I am so sorry. I thought you were my enemy. I am so sorry," he repeated, again, and again.

Armandus uttered more words which were nearly drowned out by his mother's screaming in the distance.

"Milord, what did he say?"

Milord could barely translate because he was so choked up.

"He said…he said, 'You killed my father also.'"

Soldiers on the porch attempted in vain to console Adelheide, but she was beyond solace. Under uncanny power, fueled by immeasurable grief, she broke away from them and ran to her dying son. Rafferty and Milord stood, rigidly braced, as she charged them maniacally, screaming and crying. She pushed them away as she fell, almost on top of Armandus.

"My son, my son! What have they done to you?" she said in a gar-bled speech that Milord was unable to translate. Armandus moaned as she rubbed his face with trembling hands, painting a bizarre, bloody mask that covered his features.

"I'm sorry, Sarge, she broke away from us," said a shaken Corporal as he and his comrades arrived, panting from their efforts to catch the woman.

They seized her, gently as she allowed, and dragged her away from Armandus. She became calm for a moment as she beseeched Rafferty in a childlike voice, offering him the brown sack she had clutched throughout the ordeal.

"What is she saying, Milord?" said Rafferty sorrowfully.

"She says to make sure he eats his lunch," replied Milord, gazing toward nothing, wishing he were anywhere but in this place.

Consumed with grief, Rafferty clung desperately to the boy, whose grip on his hand was loosening.

"I am sorry, son! God, I am sorry," he yelled in the boy's ear.

Armandus spoke another phrase, released his grip on Rafferty's hand, and of life on this plane.

As members of the patrol attempted in vain to console Adelheide, who was clutching at her chest, their comrades completed their search of the property, and Rafferty and Milord attended to the boy, cleaning him up with wet snow, covering him with a blanket from Milord's backpack. Milord knelt in the snow, shoulders sagging.

Rafferty placed a hand on his shoulder.

"What did she call him?"

"Armandus."

"I'll never forget this day—this moment; I hope you can get over it," said Rafferty.

"I won't. And I hope you get comfort from what he said," replied Milord.

Rafferty stared dumbly as Milord relayed Armandus' last words.

"He said 'You are forgiven,'" said Milord, as he buried his face in his hands.

With keen eyes, Reynard witnessed the tragedy from the depths of the dark forest, blessedly unaware of the sadness, unknowing that his life had been spared by the kindness of a gentle young man, unconcerned that the incident had changed Bowman Rafferty's life forever.

In contrast to the idiom, hell did freeze over for the thousands of Allied troops, including 189,000 casualties, who suffered unimaginable horrors of the coldest winter in Europe's history; grisly deaths; stiff, frozen bodies chiseled from their foxholes; frostbitten, black feet and fingers amputated; trenches littered with mismatched limbs belonging to the mercifully deceased. Bowman Rafferty witnessed it all. But thanks to the arrival of Patton's 3rd Army, and despite all that he'd endured, months before Germany's defeat, Bowman exited the European Theater without a scratch on his body. His spirit was sorely wounded, though; open wounds rotting with the grotesque memories of those he'd killed, and especially, of the innocent boy that he slaughtered that dismal January day; the blood-saturated snow; the agony inflicted on that wretched woman; the benediction given to him by the boy he murdered. Somehow, that godly sanction, "Tu es pardonné," did not serve to comfort him. In his dreams, he got what he deserved from the boy, who swore at him and spat upon him, flinging curses with his dying breath. That's what he deserved. When he prayed, which was often, he prayed to Armandus thanking him for undeserved absolution. Afterward, he prayed to God, asking for release from his torment. God did not choose to honor his request right away. But ultimately an emissary was dispatched, and her tender ministrations eased Bowman's pain immensely.

Chapter 2

THE RESISTANCE

It was a miserable day for the 8th Air Force. It was a nightmare for Mortsel, a town near Antwerp. Allied bombers were dispatched from England to take out the state-of-the-art Messerschmitt plant there. Hindered by antiaircraft fire and the agile Messerschmitts of the Luftwaffe, bombers hit only two of their designated targets. Disastrously, twenty-four metric tons of bombs fell on civilian areas of towns—causing nearly one thousand civilian casualties.

Captain Lowell Calhoun could only guess at the extent of the carnage down below. His B-17 Superfortress was pocked from shrapnel distributed by a storm of antiaircraft fire, and all of his concentration was focused on guiding the lumbering behemoth back to the Netherlands. He had lost contact with the airmen in the back of and beneath the plane, assuming they were dead or wounded. He watched, horrified, as his fighter escort, an RAF Spitfire, was blown out of the sky, leaving him vulnerable to the flock of Messerschmits that wheeled and darted at the clumsy bombers like a gang of crows pecking at a hawk, riddling the aircraft with machine-gun fire. Several bombers plummeted from the sky that day, some within the horror-struck vision of Calhoun and his copilot, Lt. Donald Wellman. With the fighter escort dispatched, and sensing a kill, the pilot of the Messerschmitt BF 109 dove at the Superfortress, guns blazing. The cabin became an angry beehive of buzzing bullets, ricocheting and thunking noisily off of the super-structure, sadly embedding their fatal stings into the lieutenant's skull, others piercing Calhoun's shoulder and carving a deep wound in his forehead. The last thing Lowell Calhoun witnessed, through a veil of blood, were the pointed noses of the fighters, and the bright strobe flashes of machine-gun fire.

He awakened in severe pain. Blood had caked and dried over his eyes and he assumed that he was blinded. It was griddle-hot in the cabin, which was filling with smoke, and he could make out crimson flickers through his glued-shut eyelids. Was this the hell he'd been forced to believe in as a child? He heard muffled voices in the distance. Were they Beelzebub's minions, coming to spirit him away to some boiling cauldron. With his one good hand, he struggled to remove his sidearm from his shoulder holster. After several tries, he managed to place the barrel of the Colt 1911 .45 beneath his chin. "Not today, mon ami," said a gruff voice as the pistol was swatted from his hand. "They speak French in hell," he thought as he slipped into exquisite unconsciousness.

The pain shook him to his senses. "Wake up, Lowell, you got some hurtin' to do," it demanded.

"My crew?" he asked. A young woman, with liquid brown eyes, bent into his view.

"I am sorry. They are gone, Captain," she said in English, awash in tones of beautiful French. He started to close his eyes in grief for his comrades, but was afraid that he would never open them again.

"It took us about an hour to clean the blood out of your eyes. It was, how you say, about an eench thick," she said as other faces appeared in his clearing view. A handsome young man's head appeared, parting the crowd of faces.

"Catrin, how is Captain Calhoun doing?"

He continued before she had a chance to answer.

"My comrades and I are your friends. We are one of many Belgian resistance groups. We are called the Comet Line. Have you heard of us?"

Calhoun had. And he was relieved, although his physical pain, and the deep sorrow he felt for his bosom comrades, dampened the feeling.

"Yes. You are going to get me to safety," he said with great difficulty.

"Yes, but first we are to get you comfortable, no?"

"I would appreciate that very much," said Calhoun, as the young man jabbed the needle into his thigh.

Soon the pain, mostly all of it, dissipated in a wave of soothing drug-fueled warmth.

"You feeling better now?" said the young man as he dressed Calhoun's wounds.

"Yeah. Keep that stuff comin'. What's your name, Medic?"

His words were met with soft laughter and unintelligible comments around the room. The girl in the beret appeared, her wet brown eyes smiling.

"He is a doctor, Captain," and she gazed at the young man with more than admiration in her beautiful eyes.

"My name is Christophe Peeters, and this beautiful lady is Catrin de Jonge. We are in the process of becoming doctors. And you, Captain Calhoun, are helping us fulfill our residencies," said the doctor, as, with the help of morphine, Calhoun was able to close his eyes and sleep.

Under their care, Calhoun healed quickly, and when he was able, was spirited from farmhouse to farmhouse in the Belgian countryside. He was given new clothing, taught a little French, a little Flemish and German, issued a passport. He detected a tinge of animus from some of his rescuers, suspecting that their lightly veiled hostility was borne of the civilian casualties near Mortsel. The last time he saw Doctor Peeters, he hesitantly mentioned the resentment that was often palpable.

"I am sorry for your losses and any part I may have had in them," said Calhoun, as Christophe applied medication and a bandage on the pink hypertropic scar that slithered between the worry lines on his forehead—a lifelong reminder of this war.

"C'est la vie… C'est la guerre," said Christophe, remembering the horror and sadness he felt when he learned of his family's deaths at the hands of the Allied powers.

"Now, your friends are waiting to take you on a holiday," he said, patting Calhoun softly on his uninjured shoulder.

"Can you tell me where I am going?"

"I can only tell you that Spain is beautiful at this time of year. And England is even more so as the spring settles in."

Calhoun smiled deeply.

"And so is South Carolina."

"What is this Sout Caroleena?"

"It's my home. Where my wife and son and all of my relatives are waiting for me," he said, his eyes bright with tears.

There was a command from the top of the steps. Christophe hugged the man gently.

"Bon voyage. Veel geluk," said Christophe, as Calhoun's heels disappeared from view on the stairwell. He was one of seven hundred downed airmen that were saved by the Comet Line and other Belgian resistance groups in the last phases of the war.

Belgium hadn't fully recuperated from the German occupation of WWI when it was again occupied in WWII. And despite King Leopold's surrender to the Germans without consulting the government, the government in exile fought on as best they could. The liberation of Belgium in 1944 was paid for with an extravagant price in human lives—including over 19,000 resistance fighters, who supplied the allies with intelligence on troop movements, destroyed key railways, sheltered downed airmen, and were executed for their patriotism by the Gestapo. Despite the devastation, the end of the war was met with jubilation by many.

Catrin looked up at the busy feet walking by their basement apartment in Antwerp. It had been a while since people moved about so briskly and in so many numbers. She was packing the last of her meager wardrobe in the suitcase when Christophe sidled up behind her.

"I am going to miss you. How long are you staying with your relatives in Ostend?"

"That depends on how long you will stay in the Ardennes," she said, as she closed the cheap and battered cardboard suitcase and snapped the locks shut.

"Only a few days, then I'll return to Antwerp, hopefully, to you," he said, kissing the back of her neck, which sent shivers down her spine.

"I will meet you in about a week. If I get here sooner, I will busy myself at the hospital."

"I hope we can return at the same time. I don't ever want to be without you for very long," he said, bending to tie his shoe.

"Je t'adore," she said turning to face him, but he was still on one knee.

"Oh, Christophe, I almost fell over you," she giggled.

"Will you marry me, even if I don't have a ring yet?" he said, clasping her hand tightly.

She laughed and pulled him to his feet, a single tear coursing down her lovely face.

"I would marry you even if you never gave me a ring," she said as she hugged his neck tightly.

"You will have a beautiful ring, I promise," he said as she refused to relinquish her grip on him.

"Je t'adore," she whispered in his ear.

"I live for you," he replied softly.

Chapter 3

VISITING FLEUR AND ROOS

After weaving through the rubble-strewn streets of St. Vith, the battered Citroën bounced and slid along the primitive roads that wound through hills and thick forests of the Ardennes. Christophe was in no hurry to get home, and he stopped occasionally in the midst of the beeches and oaks to take in the flora and fauna of the region. Once he spied a huge boar disappearing into the forest; later he saw a lumbering sow, with four little piglets in tow, scampering comically through a meadow. He cut off the primitive main road onto a leaf-canopied lane that emerged into a clearing, beside a springhouse on the edge of an eddying creek. Beyond, on a small rise, was his home. He wasn't eager to reach his destination, and he exited the car, preferring to walk in order to make the trip a little longer. He had not walked far when he heard a snarl, and beheld a muscular Malinois racing at him at terrific speed. He knew that he couldn't make it back to the car before the Belgian shepherd took him down, so he squatted on his haunches and looked at the ground, in a posture of submission. But the dog kept on coming, bent on protecting his home. Suddenly, there was a shrill whistle and a shout, and the dog skidded to a stop.

"Patrasche! Stay," cried the old man from the porch. The once-ferocious animal now seemed to smile as it ran back to its master.

Christophe stood hesitantly.

"Is that you, Uncle Guillaume?"

"It is me, my Christophe, I am coming to you. Patrasche will not harm you," yelled the old man as the dog herded him toward the young man.

As his uncle approached, Christophe was chagrined to see how he had aged throughout these few years.

The dog, merry now, frolicked around them as they embraced.

"You remind me so much of my sister," cried the old man, his eyes and nose dripping.

"Come, we will have some supper and some beer, yes?"

"Yes, and talk of old times. I will bring the car up. Make sure Patrasche remembers me," he laughed. The old man waved his hand in the air in observance of the remark as he hobbled back to the house.

They had skipped dinner, and proceeded directly to the alcoholic beverages. Bottles of every kind and description littered the kitchen table: Duvel Blonde, Flemish Brown and Red Ale, Stout. There was also a crock of Genever and shot glasses. Guillaume was getting drunk, and Christophe was developing a heavy buzz.

"I am sorry for serving you so many different kinds, Nephew. The brands are not as plentiful as before the war and I had to buy what I could get at the time."

"They are all quite tasty, but I am afraid my stomach will be in revolt tomorrow if I don't have something to eat," laughed Christophe, and his stomach growled to punctuate the remark.

Guillaume swayed dangerously as he got up from the table and wobbled in the direction of the pantry, then, to the icebox. He made several trips, carrying a loaf of bread, a hunk of Gouda, a charcuterie board with pate and smoked ham, and a bowl containing greens.

"Your cousin, Jolien, sent these with her best wishes," he said, handing Christophe a plate and eating utensils.

"Be sure to enjoy the salade liégeoise, it is lovely," said the old man, as he dished heaps of the greens, beans, bacon, and onions slathered in vinegar onto Christophe's plate. They ate ravenously, and in silence. Finally, Christophe scooted himself back from the table, an overture to continue the conversation.

"My compliments to Jolien," he said, burping softly. Guillaume ignored the remark as he cut to the chase.

"Have you visited the graveyard?"

"No, I plan to do that tomorrow," said Christophe, not wanting to broach the subject.

"Thankfully, it was untouched by the war and remains in good shape. I take care of that," said Guillaume who was revisiting the beer. After a couple of gulps, his eyes watered heavily again.

"Did you hear what your blessed brother said to the American that shot him?"

Christophe choked on his answer.

"Yes, I heard in a letter that was sent to me by Mamma before she died. He said 'you are forgiven.' That would be a typical response from sweet Armandus. He was a saint," said Christophe, who had returned also to the alcohol. They were quiet for some time, each wrapped up in their personal thoughts of beautiful Armandus and others taken by this senseless conflict. Christophe finally spoke on a new note.

"Thank you, Uncle, for everything you have done. I have some other favors to ask of you, and I want to repay you for your kindness and allegiance to our family."

"Anything. What is it that you want?"

"I want you to take whatever you need from this place, including the horses. Then, sell the farm. I will split the money with you and use my share to pay for the rest of my education."

"How about the furniture, photos, mementos of your childhood, and of your family?"

"You keep them. My memories are right here," said Christophe, thumping his chest with his fist.

"Then you will be returning to Antwerp, to the university?"

"I have already returned and am planning on establishing a practice there in the future."

The old man stood, and holding on to the table edge for balance, inched over to Christophe, bent, and kissed him on the cheek.

"I gladly accept your request," he said. He didn't bother to say good night as he slowly made his way to the staircase.

Christophe was awakened by a furious headache and the slamming of a door. He peered out of the window and saw the figure of Guillaume wavering slowly through the fog across the field, Patrasche gamboling happily ahead of him.

The kitchen table was cleaned of all reminders of the night before, with the exception of a Genever jug that weighted down a piece of wrinkled paper. There was a message, written shakily in the palsied, arthritic hand of the old man:

Have fed the horses and they are looking forward to seeing you. Have gone to Jolien's. She has breakfast and headache powders. Join us if you'd like. She lives in the house of your grandmother. Guillaume

Christophe tried to focus on the old man's humor and his resiliency. But his headache squelched his thoughts. He made himself a pot of black coffee, nibbled on a stale croissant, and eventually, the headache waned. Later, he rummaged through his backpack for some work pants, a flannel shirt, and a light jacket. On his way out, he stepped into a pair of mud-caked Wellingtons beside the door, and made his way across the springtime mud to the barn. The horses started whinnying as he advanced, perhaps sensing a sweet reunion. They neighed and stomped their huge feet as he neared them, and their soulful eyes shone with love and remembrance of him.

"Fleur! Roos! It's me, Christophe," he said, rubbing their thick necks and manes, nuzzling their noses with his own. Although they'd been fed recently, he slid half-full oat bags over their noses as he hitched them to a cart.

"I don't really need both of you to pull me in this wagon, but let's go for a walk, like old friends on a spring morning, yes?"

Roos answered with a whinny as if she knew what he was saying. Fleur concentrated on the contents of her oat bag, munching contentedly as she gazed at him deeply, with knowing eyes.

The horses seemed to enjoy the walk, tossing their heads and snorting to one another, for the cart and its contents, Christophe, were feather-light to them. They made their way through the muddy fields and onto a path covered with spruce nettles that meandered through the forest. Motes of fog and leaf dust danced on pale shafts of sun that stabbed through the giant oaks, spruce, and beech trees, and the animals started once as a red fox darted across their path. "Whoa, Roos, Fleur, it's only Reynard," said Christophe in a comforting voice. Finally, they came to a clearing: a manmade meadow that was the resting place of loved ones, old and new. It was mowed nicely; gravestones were cleaned of moss; storm-strewn branches and twigs were nonexistent on the grounds, which were raked impeccably.

"Good job, Guillaume," said Christophe in a reverent whisper, as he made his way through the garden of stone. Some of the stones were ancient, crumbling, patronyms and given names made indistinguishable by time. Other names that could be read were of French, Flemish, and German ancestry, but most of the stones bore the names of the Peeters family and the De Waeles, his mother's maiden name. The fog was lifting as he stopped in a suddenly sun-drenched corner of the meadow, where three relatively fresh graves were evident: tented mounds of dirt surrounded by the flat, grassy resting places of long dead ancestors. He traced the headstones with his fingers, reading to himself the simple bios of Sander, who was crushed beneath a wall, and Adelheide, who had died of heart failure two weeks subsequent to Armandus' death. He was moved to tears. Afterward, he knelt in the wet grass that bordered his beloved brother's grave and read aloud:

Armandus, son of Sander and Adelheide, brother of Christophe.
Tragically taken from us.
Born June 10, 1928. Died January 4, 1944.

"Sixteen; he was so good," said Christophe, and his knees popped loudly in the quietness as he stood to leave. Stoic and hardened by his experiences in the war, Christophe attempted to contain his grief as he walked numbly back to the horses. And he remembered.

He was always enamored with the thought of being a doctor, and even at a young age, he treated all of the farm animals for a wide array of maladies. He was quick to doctor family members also, especially his younger brother, who seemed to experience his share of injuries.

"Now this is going to hurt a little bit, Armandus," he said as he drenched the wound in merbromin in preparation for stitching up his brother's foot. Roos had stepped on the boy's foot, and the weight of the horse split it open, forming a wide gash.

"I'll be brave," said Armandus, and he made not a sound as Christophe deftly sewed up the wound with his mother's needle and thread.

"That was excellent, didn't hurt at all," said Armandus, tears rolling down his cheeks.

The sight and sound of his dear brother's pain angered Christophe, who stood and slapped Roos hard on the neck.

"Dumb, clumsy animal," he yelled and she backed up as he started to strike her once more.

"No! Don't hit her again!" yelled Armandus, as he struggled to get to his feet.

"Why shouldn't I?" snapped Christophe.

"Because I love her," said Armandus, eyes pleading.

"Very well. I'll look at that foot again tonight. In the meantime, keep it clean," said Christophe as he left the barn.

"Christophe! I love you too," yelled Armandus after him.

By the time he'd reached the horses, Christophe was in deep tears. Before he got into the wagon he kissed Roos on the neck. And as they pulled away, he spoke aloud.

"I love you, and I always will," he said, and he turned the team around, their muted hoof beats barely heard on the spruce-nettle-covered path as the unadorned cortege made its way through the silent forest.

BOOK 2

TENNESSEE

Chapter 4

ROSALEE, LITTLE BOY, AND FAT MAN

Rosalee Drummond, a child born of crushing poverty in the mining community of Briceville, Tennessee, felt blessed to obtain a job at the Clinton Engineering Works, a 60,000-acre gated community, just south of her hometown which was nestled in the foothills of the Cumberlands. She really wasn't sure what the Manhattan Project was all about, and was warned not to ask when she was assigned a job at one of the four plants. "What you see here…when you leave here… let it stay here!" said her supervisors numerous times, perhaps every day, and she, along with most of her seventy-five thousand coworkers faithfully adhered to that oft-repeated caution. Rosalee, young and unmarried, went home every evening, but many of the employees— construction workers, scientists, plant workers, and their families— were housed in prefabricated homes, built on an average of one home every thirty minutes, most of which lined a six-mile stretch bordering a wide, extremely muddy, and rutted avenue. Rosalee, who possessed excellent typing and other administrative skills, was a strong right arm in assisting social workers in assigning these homes to families. She loved her job and the vibrant beehive ambience that permeated the isolated seventeen-mile valley woven through by parallel rows of sharp ridges. Rosalee received gratification in seeing the results of her work come to culmination on a daily basis, unlike the many laborers who did not reap the fruits of their labors for a lengthy period.

If the canteen was viewed from above, it would have evoked the vision of a bustling ant farm, as thousands of employees filtered through the cafeteria lines chatting, laughing, and joking with the servers. The drone of their conversations, the clattering of silverware, and the noises associated with occasional kitchen mishaps echoed throughout the mammoth hall, providing a not-unpleasant background that mimicked the effervescence of happy people, all working together with a devotion to a common cause: creating weapons-grade uranium for an atomic bomb. But at this juncture they were unaware of their critical mission; they were unaware that their exertions would end the war and save the world.

He noticed her immediately as he left the cashier's stand: petite, auburn hair upswept and held in place by a colorful headband, with inviting wisps and tendrils of hair trailing at her neck; a well-worn but clean and pressed suit jacket with square shoulders, modeled after utility clothes produced during World War II; a narrow-hipped skirt that ended just below her knee; and below her knees, prettily turned ankles. As fate would have it, there was an empty seat directly across from her.

"Is this seat taken, ma'am?" he said, hesitating at the chair.

"Actually, I was saving it for my friend, Sarah," said Rosalee, who was taken by the rugged good looks of the man, but, shy and countrified, she was horrified of having to share conversation with him.

"Sorry. I'll try to find another seat somewhere," he said as he awkwardly turned to go.

"Sit down, son. Sarah's at the other end of the table. You didn't see her, did you, Rosalee?" said the older woman who was seated at Rosalee's elbow.

You nosey old biddy, thought Rosalee, who scrambled to regroup.

"I'm sorry, sir, here, sit down," she said, her face as crimson as the beets on her plate.

He smiled a generous smile.

"Why, thank you, ma'am. Please call me Bowman; Bowman Rafferty."

"Nice…nice to meet you, Bowman," she said, staring down at her plate.

Her posture gave him an excellent opportunity to observe her delicate features, especially her thick eyelashes.

"Her name is Rosalee. Rosalee Drummond. My name is Wanda. Where do you work, son?" said Wanda, cherishing the prospect of playing matchmaker.

Bowman held his hand up, as he'd just consumed a large bite of mashed potatoes. When he had swallowed, he answered.

"I'm on one of the work crews, building houses for folks; I guess I should say 'assembling houses' since they are all pre-fabricated," he said, taking a sip of water.

Wanda laughed and elbowed Rosalee, who almost fell off her seat.

"Well, Bowman, you and Rosalee are workin' on the same project!"

"You mean to tell me you work on a building crew?" he said, tell-tale mischief sparking in his twinkling blue eyes.

"No, no, I work in the office, helping to assign homes for people to move in," she said, finally managing the courage to look him in the face; not just a handsome face, a kind, intelligent face.

"As a matter of fact, she may have assigned a house for you and your wife; got any kids?" said Wanda, demonstrating her proficiency at baiting.

"She may have. I'm not married, but during the week, I live in a dorm for single men and I go home on the weekends," he said, playing the game with finesse.

Rosalee decided it was time to speak, if only to shut Wanda's big mouth.

"Where's home, Mr.…I mean, Bowman?" she said almost tersely, firing a shot-across-the bow glance at Wanda, who smiled sweetly at her.

"I live on a farm right now with my daddy, just north of here, outside of Harrogate, Tennessee."

"You just got out of the service, didn't you, Bowman?" said Wanda in a tender, almost sorrowful tone.

"How did you know?"

"Lots of young men have mustered out lately, including my son; he was a Marine and he's living with me and my husband, up the valley, just over the line from Campbell County into Claiborne County."

Wanda expected him to ask about her son's regiment, division, anything that had to do with a comrade-in-arms. But he skirted those issues.

"It's purty up the valley, ain't it?"

"We love it, especially since Billy's come home. Where did you...?"

He scooted his chair back noisily, picking up his tray as he got up.

"Sorry, have to go. It was nice meeting you ladies, and I hope to see you again," he said, speaking with emphasis, riveting his eyes on Rosalee as he spoke.

Still miffed, Rosalee spoke quietly to Wanda.

"How did you know he was just out of the service?"

"The sorrow and secrets hidden in those beautiful eyes. It's like they are saying, 'I know something terrible that you don't know, but I'm not allowed to tell you.' Billy has the same look in his precious eyes," said Wanda, her own eyes filling with tears.

All of Rosalee's displeasure with Wanda melted away and she reached over to pat the distraught woman's hand.

"It's alright, Wanda. God will heal them in time."

Wanda dabbed at her eyes with a frilly handkerchief that she kept tucked in her ample bosom.

"I know, honey. But remember, we are the strongest instruments of our Creator."

He was seeking her out, but she was looking for him too. Her tiny hand shot up in the air, and her quiet voice barely rose above the din when she saw him.

"Hey, Bowman! Over here, I saved you a seat," she said, and she was trembling when he accepted her invitation.

"Thanks, Rosalee. This place is packed today," he said and stopped himself from touching her shoulder.

He glanced at her meager lunch: a peanut-butter sandwich, looking forlorn on a piece of waxed paper.

"What you got there, Rosalee?"

"It's a peanut-butter sandwich. I try not to pay for lunch a couple of days a week, just to save a little. I'm really not hungry today; besides, I'm not too fond of peanut butter," she laughed.

He knew she was hungry, knew by the way she looked longingly at his plate.

"I love peanut butter. You like chopped steak, mashed taters and gravy, and these little bitty cabbages?" he said gesturing at his plate, which was heaped full of victuals. Before she could answer, he grabbed her peanut-butter sandwich and slid his plate and silverware over to her.

She was moved by his act of chivalry, and made a weak attempt at refusing his offer. But he rebuffed her as he made a show of enjoying the sandwich.

"Um, this is good! Now go ahead, you eat your lunch. And you know what? On the days you can't buy lunch, you fix me a peanut-butter sandwich, and I'll trade you for whatever you want from the cafeteria line. Fair enough?"

His eyes were pleading, and she didn't have the heart to refuse him. Besides, she was starving. She reached out tentatively and touched his hand softly.

"It's a deal. Thank you, Bowman," she said sweetly as she dug in to her meal. She began to laugh.

"What's the matter?"

"These little bitty cabbages are called brussels sprouts," she giggled.

He grinned, a tiny bit of peanut butter dangling precariously from the corner of his mouth.

"I knew that, just couldn't think of the name," he said, as Rosalee lovingly wiped away the bit of peanut butter with her napkin; then they both laughed joyously.

From a couple of tables away, Wanda watched them surreptitiously.

"Do what you were made for, little woman. Let the healing begin," she said to herself. And she laughed out loud as she watched Rosalee clean up her plate.

Rosalee and Bowman's courtship blossomed quickly; they both were happier than they had been in ages. Their elation was heightened when, in May, Germany surrendered, and the war in Europe ended. But the conflict continued in the Pacific. Japan showed no signs of surrender—ever. Drastic measures were taken, measures in which the toil of employees at Clinton Electrical Works figured deeply to defeat the bellicose Nipponese.

On August 6, 1945, the B-29 Superfortress bomber the Enola Gay dropped the bomb known as "Little Boy" on the largest city in western Honshu, the largest island in Japan. The atomic blast ultimately killed 166,000 residents of Hiroshima. Three days later, after three unsuccessful passes due to drifting smoke and clouds, the B-29 Bockscar abandoned its target, the city of Kokura. The mission was redirected to the city of Nagasaki, where the payload, called "Fat Man," was dropped. "Fat Man" was ultimately responsible for taking over 80,000 lives. Although botched at first, the mission was reported successful, and Japan surrendered soon after the devastation.

Wildly desirous to end the war, American patriots declined to debate ethical justification of killing over a quarter of a million civilians in a matter of days. To many, the number was defensible as reparation for the deaths and maiming of their loved ones on the battlefields of Europe and in the Pacific, and for the deep sacrifices made on the home front. Many of those who had witnessed firsthand the brutality, futility, and stupidity of war kept their mouths shut, recalling vivid images of death and unimaginable agony, and as the multitudes cried "victory at any cost," the spiritually wounded prayed fervently for their own souls, the souls of the collateral slain—of their comrades and yes, even their enemies.

Rosalee stood on her desk, tapping a nail into the Cemesto wall in her office.

"Will you hand me that frame, Wanda?" she asked over her shoulder.

Wanda complied with the request and stood back, eyeballing the project.

"That looks good, Rosalee. Now, you can help me hang mine. I'd kill myself if I tried to get up on my desk."

Now that the war was over, employees of the Clinton Electrical Works proudly displayed certificates awarded them for their diligence and the vital part they played in winning the war. They were proud to wear shoes dirtied from trudging the muddy streets; it identified them as some of the people who held the distinction of saving the world.

Rosalee kept her job in the housing department, which helped in obtaining one of the vacated homes on Florida Street. That's where Bowman carried her across the threshold after they were married.

"Oak Ridge," as it was now known, was labeled a high-tech research facility. Because of his service, Bowman was promoted to a well-paying job, playing a small role in producing plutonium from uranium, plying long rods to insert uranium slugs into the 12,000 openings of a graphite reactor. Using the GI Bill, he also attended school in the evenings, working toward a degree in agronomy, which he planned to teach, hopefully at a college level, one day.

Chapter 5

MEETING ELA MAE AND RAY

Bowman was jumpy as a cat as they drove northward to Lake City, toward Briceville.

"Damn it! Get off the road if you don't know how to drive!" he yelled at the old truck in front of them. A farmer's weathered old hand snaked out of the window and motioned for him to pass, which he did. Rosalee scooted over next to him.

"What's the matter with you, honey? Somebody been pokin' sticks in your cage?" she said, rubbing his shoulder lovingly.

"You know what's the matter, Rosalee. I'm afraid your daddy is going to kick my ass for getting married to you without asking him."

"Well, Mamma's not too happy either. But I think she's the one you have to worry about," said Rosalee, who was pretty jittery about the meeting herself. They had fled to Georgia on a Saturday morning and become man and wife at nine in the evening. The ceremony, held in the parlor of a preacher's home, was brief, with the preacher's wife playing "Oh Promise Me" on the out-of-tune upright.

"Are you'uns both willin' to give your hand to the one whose heart you hold?" said the parson, and just like that, they were married.

Bowman had met Rosalee's mother, Ela Mae, on one occasion during his and Rosalee's brief courtship. She was gentle, like Rosalee; loved to garden, which was good because she raised five daughters on meager earnings; and you could tell by her flashing eyes when she wasn't pleased about something that she didn't take any crap.

"You mean to tell me that some French people warn't very nice to you durin' the war? Why you liberated them, God bless their hearts," said Ela Mae, who might as well have said, "Those ungrateful sons of bitches; screw them!"

It was on a Saturday when that first visit took place, and Rosalee's father, Raymond, who was sixty years old and suffering from a myriad of maladies, was still working at the mine, so he wasn't present. Soon after that visit, Bowman and Rosalee, in a fit of love and passion, decided to get hitched. It took them almost three weeks to break the news to their parents, and now, it was time to face the music.

When they arrived at the little house, they were disappointed to see a large assortment of cars and trucks parked in the yard and precariously on the steep lane leading to the home.

"Oh land sakes! It looks like they've invited my sisters to watch the slaughter," said Rosalee, as they parked crossways across the dead end at the end of the lane.

Children of every age and gender raced to greet them while adults sat on the porch. The young women, all of who resembled Rosalee in some fashion, smiled sweetly as they followed the youngsters out to the road to greet them. Her oldest sister, Lola, was the first adult to greet them with a big hug. Her eyes twinkled with humor, and possibly a little trepidation, as her smile widened and she spoke to Rosalee through gritted teeth.

"Mamma's fit to be tied. She and Daddy are sittin' under the oak tree in the shade. You might go straight to 'em," she said.

There were many other adults sitting with the older couple, but they departed quickly to the porch when Rosalee and Bowman approached. Raymond didn't stand when they confronted him.

"Give me some sugar, Rosalee. I'd stand for ye, but I'm down on my back today," he said as she bent to kiss him, then moved to her mother, who sat rigidly with her arms folded.

"It's good to see you, Daughter. Haven't seen you in a while," she said icily, her eyes flashing.

"We were just cookin' dinner. Why don't you come in the kitchen

and let Daddy and Bowman talk?" said Lola, the self-appointed ar-
bitrator at the scene. Lola and Rosalee chatted amiably as Ela Mae
followed them stiffly to the house. Bowman sat reticently next to
Raymond, and was secretly glad that today he was encumbered with
a bad back. Raymond cut to the chase.

"Well, I heered through the grapevine that you and my youngest
daughter run off and got murried? That so?"

"Yes, sir. Went to Georgia and got married by a preacher down
there," he said, eyeing Raymond's overalls for the outline of a pistol.

"Well, Lordy mercy! Why in the world didn't you let us know? All
of air daughters have got murried in the church, and we was hopin'
that Rosalee would too someday," said Raymond, his thin voice rising. Then, he went into a coughing fit. There was some movement on
the porch, and mumbling. Bowman wished the old man would stop
coughing, fearing that a squad from the porch brigade would decide
to come to his defense.

"I'm sorry, Mr. Drummond. It wasn't very thoughtful of us. But
Rosalee said that if you would like, you all can have a reception for
us," said Bowman, more nervous than he had ever been in battle, except for that one time.

"Well now, that's up to Ela Mae, if she ever gits her hackles down,"
said Raymond, and he laughed out loud, which caused more mumbling from the porch. Raymond changed the subject.

"Ela Mae tells me that you just returned from the war."

"Yes sir, it's been a couple of years now."

"Where did you fight?"

"I was in the Battle of the Bulge; France and Belgium, mostly."

The old man leaned forward, wincing in pain, but friendlier in
demeanor.

"Did ye give them Germans hell?"

"That place was hell, for everyone. But we sent 'em packing," said
Bowman.

Raymond's eyes looked far into the past.

"Ever heered of Black Jack Pershing? Well, I was jest a young'un when I fought under him with the American Expeditionary Forces in the Argonne."

Before Bowman could answer, Raymond continued, as if reliving a dream.

"Ela Mae tells me that you said some of them French people warn't vury nice to be around."

"Some of them can be pretty arrogant..."

"What's that mean?"

"You know, kind of uppity."

Raymond laughed again, causing quite a stir on the porch.

"I fought right next to them boogers against those Germans for nigh on to forty-seven days in a row. The enlisted men, like me, was pretty good fellers; they called themselves 'poilu'; but their officers were, what did you call it?"

"Arrogant."

"Right. Real uppity. Was you an officer?"

"No sir, I was a sergeant."

"I was a private. Took care of the mules," said Raymond, and he groaned as he struggled to sit up straight.

"Well, son, I'd appreciate it if you called me Ray, or Dad. Now, help me up, and we'll go to the house and have some dinner."

It seemed that the porch people were ready to applaud as Bowman helped Raymond out of the chair.

As he was assisting Raymond up the steps, the old man looked at him and winked.

"If Ela Mae's taters taste funny to ye, spit 'em out."

"I'll do that, Ray," said Bowman, quite relieved.

Dinner turned out to be a happy affair. Ela Mae's malice had melted away in the company of her daughters, especially Rosalee, whom she adored. Bowman learned a lot from his brothers-in-law, who'd learned long ago to keep their mouths shut, especially in matters of the heart, in the presence of the Drummond sorority.

"So, how you like workin' at Oak Ridge?" said Bob, Lola's husband.

"It's pretty good. But I'm going to school to become a teacher," said Bowman, as Rosalee gave his leg an encouraging pat under the table.

"Teacher? What are you goin' to teach?" said Darlene's husband, Sam.

"Well, I hope to teach agriculture."

Three of the brothers-in-law clapped in approval.

"That's good! Maybe you can teach these two goofballs somethin' about growin' crops," said Sam, jerking his thumb at his two in-laws.

"You ever growed stuff?" said Raymond.

"I was brought up on a farm, and my daddy still farms, along with my brother," said Bowman, as someone passed him a bowl of potatoes.

"Well, good for ye, son. You got a leg up on it," said Raymond as Bowman dished some potatoes into his plate.

"I hope so, when I finish school, we'd like to start a family," he said and grimaced as Rosalee squeezed his leg hard under the table.

Ela Mae's eyes flashed as she frowned.

"What's wrong with startin' one now?" she said in a no-nonsense tone.

Raymond laughed aloud.

"How's them taters taste, son?" he said, and everyone with the exception of Ela Mae laughed along with him.

Bowman and Rosalee, both intensely relieved that the day had turned out so well, laughed a lot on their trip home.

"How did them taters taste, honey?" she giggled.

"They were good, better than I thought they would be," he said as he slowed to allow a semi onto the main road.

"I get the feeling that nobody crosses your mother, that so?"

"I think you're right—but it's not out of fear, it's out of love and respect for her," said Rosalee.

"Did your mother rule the roost?" she said.

"No way. My dad has always been in charge, and I actually felt as though my mother suffered for it," he said, fearing that he had said too much.

"What do you mean, 'suffered for it'? Did he beat her?"

"No, he saved that for my brother. But I guess he wore her down verbally."

"Why did he treat your brother so badly?"

"Bernard is good inside—a tender heart, like you. But my father is one of these people who sees goodness as weakness, and he despises weakness," said Bowman, as the Anderson County sign came into view.

"But you're good, honey, why didn't he get on you?"

"I don't know, honey. I guess it's because life has been kinder to me, and I'm not as good as Bernard," he said as they pulled into their yard.

Rosalee knew at that moment that Bowman didn't care too much for his father.

Their lives were blissful as they lavished tender respect on one another; he was touched by her goodness and innocence; she was enamored with his gentle strength and intrigued by the quiet thoughtfulness that ruled his expression at times.

"You're awful quiet tonight, honey; what's on your mind?" she said as they lay in bed together.

"It's a secret," he said, gently touching her cheek.

"I never had many secrets," she giggled.

"That's because you are innocent," he said, sliding his arm beneath her neck and dragging her over to his shoulder.

He felt her turn hot. She embarrassed easily, even after they had consummated their marriage.

"Actually, I'll confess. You know what my biggest secret ever was?"

"What's that?"

"The way I felt when I first saw you. It was sinful, and I don't think I'm ever going to get over it," she said and buried her head bashfully in the hollow of his neck.

"Well, I hope you don't, honey, especially after the way you acted about an hour ago."

She slapped him lightly on the arm. "Stop it, Bowman! Now you tell me about your secret."

He turned out the light, and held her closer.

"Okay, here goes," he said, and he was silent for a while, gathering courage. He began his confession by repeating the phrase that he'd memorized in French. "Tu es pardonné," he spoke, almost in a whisper. Before she could ask, he translated the phrase for her. "Those are the words he spoke and I'll never forget them," he said, and he continued. She listened intently and her compassionate heart broke for him as he related the story of Armandus' absolution. It was the first time he'd told the story of that fateful day in the dreary fog outside of St. Vith, in the blood-stained snow. She broke the long silence that followed the dreadful tale. "But you are forgiven, Bowman—by a saint. And God forgives you too," she said, noticing that his face was wet when she touched him. "I don't know if I'll ever be able to forgive myself," he said, this time burying his head in her soft little shoulder. She ran her free hand through his hair and spoke gently. "Then I'll just have to remind you to do so," she said. As he slept, she wept for her man. And she lay awake for a lengthy time, trying to decide what she could offer to dispel his torment.

Their workdays were long as they counted the minutes when they could be near one another, nestled in their simple but charming home—he at the kitchen table studying for his classes; she, tending to the household and waiting on him, loving him with every touch of her hand and every ounce of her being, as only a woman can do. She also spent a lot of time with her cross-stitching, on a project designed especially for him.

"What you workin' on, honey?" he would say as he passed her by or brought her a glass of tea occasionally.

"Just a little farm scene. See the barn, and the cows?" she'd say as he bent to kiss her, appreciative of the fact that she was lovingly mindful of his devotion for farming, and that the project was for him.

On the weekends, they would travel up the valley to Claiborne County, to his father's farm. While Bowman, his father, and brother Bernard would tend to farming matters, she would stand in the fields, watching them work (sometimes helping them) and drawing inspiration for her project as she gazed at the gorgeous panorama of the farm nestled up against the mountains near Cumberland Gap.

She continued, diligently embroidering the vista on her Aida cloth; however, the bucolic scene was to feature more than what she had completed thus far. She spent time in the library researching the phrase that was to be the centerpiece for her work.

She came home late one day to find him sitting in her chair, holding the nearly finished piece in his hands.

"This is beautiful, honey. There's an awful lot of space in the middle; are you going to put some more stuff in that space?" he said tentatively, afraid he might insult her for making the suggestion.

"No. It ain't finished. And yes, I have some more stuff to put in the middle," she laughed, throwing her arms around his neck as he stood to greet her.

She worked feverishly and secretively, mostly on the nights he attended school in Knoxville, to finish the project. Finally, it was completed.

"What you doin' up? You should be in bed, honey, it's nearly eleven o'clock," he said as he entered their home. She was bubbly as she jumped into his arms.

"I couldn't sleep. Besides, I got a surprise for you," she said, smothering his face with kisses. She took his hand.

"Now close your eyes and follow me. We're going to the bedroom."

"Hey! That sounds like just what the doctor ordered," he laughed, gladly obliging her request.

"No, silly. Well maybe later. C'mon," she laughed, tugging at his outstretched hand.

"Okay. You can open your eyes now," she said, her voice on the edge of squealing.

Bowman opened his eyes and glanced around the room, which was lit softly.

"I'm sorry, I don't see nothing different," he said apologetically.

"Here! Let me light up the room more," she said as she yanked on the overhead light cord.

"Look!" she yelled, pointing at the wall at the foot of their bed. The object of her enthusiasm was hanging next to their dressing mirror.

The scene depicted his father's farm, the mountains, clouds, cows; and in one corner, three men were working, baling hay. Centered in the midst of the scene was the phrase "You are Forgiven" in French.

Bowman strode toward the needlepoint and examined it closely, speechless, awestruck.

"This way, you can look at it every night before you go to bed and every morning when you wake up. It's to remind you that you are forgiven by everybody, especially God, for everything you've done and for everything you do," she said, tears streaming down her face.

Bowman turned to her, his face solemn. He grabbed her around her thin waist and lifted her off her feet.

"I worship you!" he said as they tumbled onto the bed.

"So, worship me some more," she giggled, as she gave a forceful tug at his belt.

Chapter 6

JUD AND BERNARD

Judson "Jud" Rafferty loved his two sons. But he was only proud of one of them: Bowman, the eldest, the one who revered his mother and made her cry with happiness over his goodness and victory against adversity, the one who made him proud when he came marching home a war hero, and seemingly unchanged from the horrors of his experiences, which, with most of his comrades in arms, were suffered bravely in silence. Jud tried, but couldn't hide his low regard for his second son, Bernard, who never failed to disappoint him; Bernard, the primary cause of a botched marriage; Bernard, the coward who, unable to deal with the death of his beloved mother, crawled into a bottle of bourbon and was absent at her funeral. Jud was devastated by the loss of Mary too, but, with the help of Bowman, who handled all of the arrangements and articulated the eulogy with grace and dignity, he managed to survive the chaos and tragedy of losing a loved one. Jud still counted on Bernard, and relied on the mechanical maven to keep the machinery running on the farm. Bernard strived to please his father, but knew more than anyone else that he was a born misfit, and that feeling diminished the size of his shadow in his own mind, and in most everyone's estimation. His only saving grace was when his father sold some acreage and financed the purchase of his business, "Bernie's Auto Repair," the only one of its kind in Cumberland Gap, Tennessee. It was a fairly successful venture, and would have thrived more had Bernard not indulged in an occasional bender, suffered minor scrapes with the law, and been labeled "the village idiot" in some circles. Bernard feared his father, and suffered greatly over the vast rift between them. But he was bolstered by the affection shown to him by his brother, and he idolized Bowman as his champion. He also idolized Bowman's wife, Rosalee—kind, loving, and now pregnant with her first child.

Bernard hesitated as she came toward him; he put his arms behind his back, afraid he would get grease on her apron.

"Bernard! Come on in, honey, I was just about to fry some chicken," she said gaily, planting a motherly kiss on his cheek.

"Hey, Rosalee. I wasn't sure you and Bowman would be here this weekend, or I would have quit work earlier," he said as he scrubbed his hands in the kitchen sink.

"We hadn't counted on it, but your daddy called Bowman this morning and asked if he could help him fluff the hay and bale it before the rain came in."

Bernard hung his head. It was a common thing for him to do.

"I was goin' to help him, but I had a couple of radiators to put in," he said disconsolately.

Rosalee, innately cognizant of other people's pain, especially Bernard's, put a hand on his shoulder.

"Don't worry about it. You got a business to run. Besides, if it weren't for you, that old baler wouldn't be runnin' anyway."

At that moment, the clump of boots reverberated heavily on the back porch, and the noise was accompanied by the screech of the screen door.

"Boy, by the look of that sky, I think we got that hay in just in time," said Bowman as he and Jud sauntered into the kitchen.

"Well, look what the cat dragged in," said Jud cheerlessly, with a half-nod toward Bernard, who was sitting at the table. Bowman came over and hugged his brother heartily.

"How's business, Bernard? You makin' any money at the shop?"

Jud cut in before Bernard could answer.

"He could be, if he didn't lay out so much. Hell, he's not savin' any money and he don't even have to pay room and board," said Jud, as Bernard visibly cringed.

"I told you, Daddy, that I would move out; I've got an apartment right above the shop."

"Lord help, Son. If you lived by yourself, even if you lived right on top of work, you'd never get to it," said Jud. Rosalee frowned as she served them iced tea.

Thankfully, Bowman changed the topic with a smooth segue.

"Can you see Rosalee's belly? It's hard to believe she's six months pregnant," he said, surrounding her hip with his arm and gently drawing her to him.

"I could hardly tell, especially through the apron. She's as purty as she ever was," said Bernard, and Jud smiled for the first time since he'd entered the house.

"I think so too. I can remember when Mary was pregnant with Bowman. I think she was prettier then than in any time since I knowed her; you remind me a lot of her," he said wistfully.

Rosalee laughed as Bowman pulled her down on his knee.

"I wish I could have known her. I'll tell you one thing: I may not look pregnant, but I sure as heck feel like it, especially when the little thing starts kickin'."

"Almost kicked me out of bed last night," said Bowman, as Rosalee snuggled tightly against him. Bernard smiled sadly, envying their closeness.

Jud gripped the pitcher of tea with his meaty hand and poured himself another glassful.

"Bowman, how much more schoolin' do you have before you get your master's degree?"

"Just a few more months. Lord, it seems like I've been going to school for twenty years straight," he said.

"It'll pay off. And we've been blessed to have your job at Oak

Ridge," said Rosalee, as she smoothed Bowman's hair back from his forehead.

Jud frowned deeply and shook his head.

"I can't wait for you to get out of that place. They say folks who worked there are gettin' sick right and left," he said in the midst of a deep, rumbling cough.

"Speakin' of getting sick. It sounds like you're gettin' a cold, Jud," said Rosalee, leaning forward, her brow furrowed in concern.

"Ah, it's just that dust and stuff from the hay, I'll be alright," he said gruffly as Bernard spoke up.

"Heck, you've had that cough for two months," he said.

"So you're a doctor now, boy? You don't know your butt from your elbow," said Jud harshly.

"C'mon, Daddy, he's just concerned for you," said Bowman, as Jud entered another coughing fit.

"Yeah, just like he was concerned for his mother when she died," said Jud, as Bernard scooted his chair abrasively across the floor and left the table.

"There was no call for that, Daddy," said Bowman.

Jud did not reply, and sat in tortured silence, along with Bowman and Rosalee. He knew that he was wrong. And somehow, he knew that he was dying.

Winter came and departed. Jud had the flu again, and his raspy coughs echoed throughout the building. Rain fell in sheets this spring morning and it was definitely "too wet to plow," so he busied himself piddling around the barn. He and Bernard had replaced the wheel bearings on both sides of the tractor the week before. Bernard took it out for a spin, and damned if he didn't hit a deep hole, breaking the spindle. Jud could have gotten a lot of plowing done before the rains came if that dumbass had been watching where he was going. So today, he was going to repair the hitch on the baler, hoping that his son would drop by after work to help him repair the damage done to the spindle.

"He's probably sleepin' the day away. He'd better drop by and help me or I'll give him what for," grumbled Jud, as he rummaged through his toolbox for a big wrench. He felt something brush up against his leg.

"Buster, where you been, boy!" he said, as he knelt down to pet his faithful Blue Heeler. Buster was sopping wet, probably from chasing rabbits, and whistle pigs in the fields. Buster shook violently, spraying water all over Jud.

"That's okay, feller, that's what dogs do, ain't it?" chuckled Jud, and he was overwhelmed by the sudden realization that he gave his dog more leeway, and more love, than he did his son. He overturned a bucket and sat down on it, a monstrous headache assailing his brain. The formerly pleasant sound of rain beating a tattoo on the barn roof sounded like kettledrums in his ears, and cold air shrouded him.

"Damn, Buster, it ain't goin' to snow, is it?" he said as he scratched the dog's broken ear. The pounding in his head continued, accompanied by the voice of Bernard as a child, crying "I'm sorry, Daddy" repeatedly. Hot tears streamed down Jud's face.

"Bernard, Bernard. Please forgive me," he said, as he fell from his bucket seat to the floor of the barn.

Buster licked his face, perhaps in an attempt to revive him. But it was too late; too late for everything.

The family arrived early at the funeral home to pay their respects to their loved one. Bernard stood alone at the casket when they departed to prepare for the visitation. It was eerily quiet in the room, which would soon be buzzing with the muted conversations of mourners proffering their condolences and reminiscing about the deceased. He reached into the casket and smoothed back his father's hair, traced his features gently with his fingertips. He focused on the hands folded across the chest—leathery calloused hands, grown thick with hard labor; hands that had provided food on the table, put fear in the hearts of erring children; hands that had gently caressed his dying wife. Through his tears, Bernard laughed as he remembered the lyrics to a song from the musical *Oklahoma*, a favorite song of his mother, who taught music before she became ill: "Poor Jud is dead; our candlelight is dead; he's looking oh so peaceful and serene; he's laid all out to rest; his hands across his chest; his fingernails have never been so clean." Bernard bent and laid his head gently on the chest that was now devoid of a heartbeat. He wondered if that stilled heart had ever beaten in praise and love for him. And he would have been surprised to know that it had…if only once. He uttered the mantra that he'd repeated daily since childhood:

"Please forgive me, Daddy."

Bowman and Rosalee were not pleased that everything—the farm, the house, the machinery, cattle; everything—was bequeathed to them and their little boy, Durand. They knew that Bernard was fragile, and that this final slap in the face would increase the velocity of his downward spiral, and did their best to make him know that he was loved, they would be there to support him, and at the first opportunity, they would change their will to leave him everything in the case of their demise. When they arrived at the farm driving a borrowed truck, they found some of his belongings on the front porch.

"What's all of this?" said Bowman, as Bernard greeted them at the front door.

"I'm movin' my stuff to the apartment above the shop," said Bernard, as he stooped to pick up a battered lamp.

"No you ain't, boy," said Rosalee adamantly, as she snatched the lamp from his hands and stormed into the house.

Both Bowman and Bernard stood silent, their mouths agape at Rosalee's reaction to Bernard's attempted departure. Bowman finally cleaved their astonishment with a heavy sigh.

"Brother, this is a big house, a good-sized farm—too big for Rosalee, me, and the baby to handle, especially with my teaching job. We want you here—we need you here—to be a part of our little family, and to care for one another," he said as Durand, just a toddler, hugged Bernard's leg affectionately, right on cue.

Before Bernard could reply, Rosalee came bolting through the screen door and picked up a basket of clothing on the porch.

"From the looks of these clothes, they're dirty. I'll wash them before you take them back up to your room," she said, as she reentered the home.

"Actually, as far as we're concerned, the whole upstairs is yours," said Bowman. Bernard made no reply as he bent to pick up Durand and walked to the corner of the porch.

"Buddy, your Uncle Bernie is goin' to be a part of your family," he said, as the baby tugged at his ear.

They didn't have many heavy possessions, and with Bernard's help and his truck, they were moved in quickly.

"Where should we put this?" said Rosalee as she cradled the framed cross-stitch reminder.

"In our bedroom. So I can look at it every morning and every night," said Bowman. Bernard heard the thumping as they hammered a nail into the wall. As they laughed, he smiled. It was good to love someone and to know that love would be reciprocated. It was good to be family.

❧❧❧

Bernard's transformation was remarkable. His normal hangdog expression was replaced with a chin-up, look-you-in-the-eye appearance that was appreciated by his customers, who were gaining in number. Rosalee ensured that he always had creases in his trousers and clean shirts; thus his rumpled appearance was a thing of the past. He still imbibed, but only on occasion, and with the advice of his brother, maintained an aura of integrity and confidence that was noted by all. He lived for his family, especially little Durand, who idolized him—a son he never had.

Bowman had arrived home from school. The aroma of food cooking greeted him first, then, sweet Rosalee, who came down the porch steps, arms outstretched, as if she hadn't seen him for months.

"Honey, how was your day?" she said, wrapping her arms around his waist.

"Fair to middlin'. I think some of my students are actually goin' to pass this year," he answered, as they fell back against the car in their embrace.

"Where's Durand?"

"Oh, he and Bernard are out in the barn fiddlin' around with that old John Deere," she said as she led him to the house.

"Hang on, I'll call 'em for supper," she said, as she rang the bell mounted on the porch support.

Soon, they heard the animated chatter of a child, the squeak of the screen door, heavy shoes and little feet stomping about the mudroom.

"Daddy! Daddy!" yelled Durand—so much like his mother as he ran to his father with hands outstretched.

"Hold it! Hold it! Let's get them hands washed first. You don't want to get grease all over his clothes," said Bernard as he hefted the child and swung him up on the kitchen counter. He turned on the water in the sink faucet and tested it for the right temperature. Durand spoke excitedly.

"We put a new carbolater in the tractor," he squealed, as Bernard scooted him over to the sink and washed their hands.

Bowman and Rosalee beamed at the scene, proud of the sweet and fulfilling progress shared by all of them.

Chapter 7

INCIDENT AT CUDJO'S CAVE

Bowman Rafferty's life, lived mostly in the protective bosom of his small family and the sparkling, well-ordered halls of academia, was sweet. His son and wife, both of whom he adored, seemed happy and comfortable under his care in their Cumberland Mountain home. He was contented too as he labored on their successful farm, sowing the earth with seeds of knowledge gained as a serious student of agronomy. He was also blessed to share his vast understanding with students of agriculture at Lincoln Memorial University, where, after earning his PhD, he was offered an assistant professorship at the school. When his rigorous agenda rendered him unable to tend to his crops, his brother, Bernard, stepped in and covered for him. His wife, Rosalee, was his rock—an icon of virtue with a firm foothold on high moral ground. She taught him with each passing day, in the soft lilt of her voice and gentle actions, to appreciate life, and to love more deeply than he could have ever imagined. He offered up thanks for his many blessings, and he knew that he was becoming a better man through those prayers; he knew because God and Rosalee bestowed their approval on him, one way or another.

Despite the contentment Bowman enjoyed during the daylight hours, often, his sleep was interrupted by bizarre nightmares, most featuring the killing of Armandus Peeters. In the dreams, Armandus did not absolve him of his sin; he railed at him in biblical tones, condemning him to perform self-deprecating acts in atonement and penance for his transgression. Other dreams involved Armandus' mother, who groveled on the ground, pleading for Bowman to ensure that her son "eat his lunch."

"Here, honey, drink this cool water; you were having another nightmare," said Rosalee as he sat upright in their bed, sweating and trembling. She rubbed his back as he gulped down the water and set the glass shakily on the nightstand. She held him close till the shuddering subsided.

"Same dreams?" she whispered in his ear.

"Same ones. I don't think it will ever stop," he said as he slipped back beneath the covers.

"Look," she said, pointing to the cross-stitched work of art hanging on the wall. It was illuminated by a shaft of blue moonlight shining through the window.

"Isn't that beautiful? It's a sign from God," she said in a childlike voice.

"And it's a sign from you. Thank you...for everything," he said, rolling over on his side. She clung to his back until he was snoring softly. When she was sure that he was asleep, she turned on her side and snuggled up against him.

A cold rain danced on the tin porch roof and a shroud of fog enveloped the pastureland and the mountain that, on a clear day, overlooked the big valley.

The kitchen was awash in the aromas of country ham, red-eye gravy, and coffee. Bowman sipped his brew from a deep cup as he gazed out the window at basically nothing.

"This rain's holdin' the fog down."

"It'll clear as the day wears on," said Bernard, who was wolfing down his second helping of biscuits and gravy.

"I have a meeting at school tonight, Bernard. Would you mind taking Rosalee to Middlesboro this afternoon? She insists on doing some Christmas shopping, and I can't talk her out of it," said Bowman as he donned a heavy, roll-collared cardigan. Bernard was about to answer when Rosalee interrupted, flitting around Bowman like a moth—buttoning, smoothing, preening.

"My, my, don't you look good in that sweater I made you; just like a professor, I might say."

"I appreciate your efforts, especially on a day like today. It'll feel good on my way to work; I might even wear it all day, just to say you made it when somebody asks," he said, slurping the last of his coffee and setting the mug on the counter.

Bernard got up from the table and carried his dishes to the sink.

"I'll be happy to take her. Is Durand goin' too?"

"If you'd like. We can pick him up from school, if you don't mind," said Rosalee as she helped Bowman with his overcoat.

Bowman scooped up his satchel from atop the sideboard and headed for the porch.

"I'll probably be home around seven or seven thirty; be careful."

"We'll be home way before then. I've got some stew going in the Crock-Pot and there will be plenty to fill all of your bellies," she laughed.

It was one of those dreary winter days when the rain continued to drizzle and the fog hung around, waiting for something to happen. Bernard had trouble installing an alternator at his shop and was late picking up Rosalee. He pulled into the driveway and honked his horn. She was waiting on the porch, purse draped over her arm.

"Whew, it's damp out there," she said, clambering into the car, taking her plastic rain bonnet off.

"Sorry I'm late."

"That's okay, Bernard. We aren't late from picking Durand up at school," said Rosalee as she adjusted the heater controls.

Nine-year-old Durand was excited about the trip to Middlesboro. Absorbed in his enthusiasm, he stood in the rain, outside of Harrogate

Grade School, waiting on the arrival of Uncle Bernard and his mother. He grinned as the old Plymouth pulled up next to the curb.

"Get in here, boy! You tryin' to catch your death of cold?" said Bernard. Rosalee was concerned but smiled, knowing that nine-year-old boys pay no attention to the weather, especially if they are excited about something.

"Here; you sit between Uncle Bernard and me. That way, you'll get the full effect of the heater," said Rosalee, wedging him between her and Bernard, cranking up the heater fan.

"Are we going to buy Daddy a Christmas present?"

"We sure are. And maybe, we'll buy some other people presents," said Rosalee, and Bernard smiled as the boy squealed with delight.

In the days before the Cumberland Gap Tunnel was completed, travelers were obligated to drive 25 E—a three-mile section of serpentine road that twisted dangerously across the mountain into Kentucky. An average of five people a year were killed in accidents on the road, and locals named the highly travelled thoroughfare "Massacre Mountain" because of the grisly statistics.

Durand was contentedly sipping on a Nehi Orange Drink they had bought him in town, when he noticed the tourist spot they had passed on the way over the mountain. "Look, there's Cudjo's Cave! Can we go in?" yelled Durand as they reached the top of the mountain on their return trip.

"I don't think it's open, honey. Besides, the weather's getting worse and we've got to get home to Daddy," said Rosalee, leaning over the seat to talk to him.

"I hear that place is hainted with the ghosts of runaway slaves and Civil War soldiers," said Bernard, as he squinted into the fog.

"Really?" said Durand, as he leaned over the seat in front of him.

"Tell me about it, Uncle Bernard!"

Rosalee's smile turned to horror.

"No!" she shouted as eerie fog-dulled headlights flooded the car.

Bernard awakened on the roadside in horrific pain. Bloodied, he couldn't move his left arm as he crawled to what was left of the car— on its side in a deep culvert.

"Buddy, buddy! Sit still" came the words of the truck driver, his form gauzy in the fog. Bernard ignored the plea as he crawled and staggered his way to the car, led by the pitiful sounds of Rosalee's moans. She was pinned in the car, covered with shattered glass and blood when he arrived.

"Rosalee! Rosalee! We'll get you out!" he said as he frantically searched for Durand inside the car.

"Where's my boy?" she whispered in an appalling rasp.

"I'm trying to find him," screamed Bernard, as sirens were heard from down the mountain.

"Bernard!" she moaned and grasped his coat sleeve through the broken window.

"What, honey?" he cried, patting her hand, smoothing her matted hair away from her bloody forehead.

Her eyes widened, but appeared opaque in the dim light.

"Don't tell. Please don't tell!" she cried. Then, her face softened and she smiled, a broken smile.

"Durand! There you are, baby! Come here to Mamma," she whispered sweetly, attempting to extricate one of her arms from the crumbled tin-can interior of the crushed car. She reached weakly into the air. Her hand fell loosely on her chest as she died.

As he had promised, Bowman arrived home about seven thirty, and was ill at ease to find the house cold and empty. But the aroma of stew in the Crock-Pot permeated the place, taking the edge off his discomfiture. He lit a fire in the fireplace to chase the chill out of the house. And as he knelt on the hearth, some of the damp wood hissed and crackled, seeming to taunt him. He was extremely hungry, and was lured by the fragrance of the slow-cooked one-pot supper in the kitchen. Lifting the lid off the pot, he reveled in the ambrosial whiff of beef stew as it masked his face in a rush of aromatic steam. He fought the temptation to dish himself a bowl, preferring instead to wait on the arrival of his family, for whom he was beginning to worry.

"Is she your wife?" said the sheriff's deputy, as he gently took Bernard's good arm and tugged him away from the wreck and the body.

"No. She's my brother's wife. Oh God, what am I going to tell him?" cried Bernard, as another deputy approached and whispered in his comrade's ear.

"Was there another person in the car?" said the deputy tentatively.

Bernard's eyes widened with hope and then, fear.

"Durand! Durand! Is he okay? Durand!" he screamed, turning around in circles, his good arm spread wide in preparation to hug the boy to him, to comfort him, to assuage the horror the child must feel at the death of his mother.

Several ambulance personnel interrupted the tragic scene.

"We need to tend to this man, Deputy, he's hurt pretty bad, running on shock and adrenaline," said an attendant dressed in overalls.

"Come with us, buddy. We've got to get you to the hospital in Middlesboro. Lay down on this litter and we'll carry you," said the man's companions.

In his hurt, confusion, and sorrow, Bernard refused to obey them. "Where is Durand?" he cried pathetically. Then he spotted flashlight beams waving erratically on the roadway a few feet away. They were accompanied by somber voices. He staggered forward, noticing the blanket-covered form of a small person lying in the road. Blood was soaking through the blanket, and there was a broken orange Nehi bottle lying just a few feet away from the form. He gasped and the attendants caught him as he collapsed next to the litter.

Bowman had fallen asleep in his easy chair, and he was awakened abruptly by the pop of a complaining pine log. Other than the sounds of the dying fire, and the mesmerizing ticking from the grandfather clock in the hallway, it was quiet in the house. He awakened with a start as the clock gonged nine times, and concern flooded his body.

"Please, God, let them be okay," he prayed aloud as he got up from his chair, and he was relieved, almost to tears, when automobile tires were heard in his driveway. He rushed through the house, flung the porch door open, and shouted into the foggy night.

"Where in the world have you all been? I was worried to death about you," he said, laughing to show his relief along with his concern. He could barely make out the outline of the automobile in the thick ocean of fog, but he was relieved to hear footsteps crunching toward him in the gravel.

He cringed and thought his legs would give way when a sorrowful, deep male voice called to him.

"Bowman, this is Sheriff Ray. I have some bad news for you."

The funeral home in Lake City was packed inside and out. Rosalee's large immediate family took up the first three rows of seats in the chapel, weeping silently as mourners filed by the closed caskets. As usual, Lola, the oldest sister, was the authority, handing out Kleenex, shushing children, comforting both family and non-family members. She also stood with Bowman intermittently to receive visitors. Her eyes had bags beneath them, and her nose was red; all in all, the normally well-coiffed sister looked like hell, but she was holding up better than the rest of the family, especially Bowman, who was nearly catatonic in his grief.

"You alright, honey?" she said, as she held on to Bowman's arm.

"No," said Bowman, as he blandly acknowledged a visitor.

Lola nervously scanned the room for signs of Bowman's brother, and was relieved to see that he was nowhere in sight. She shivered at the thought of him showing up, especially with the hard feelings harbored by the family, and the irritation Bowman showed at the mere mention of Bernard's name.

Ela Mae was unable to stand in the receiving line, but Ray insisted, and several of the men stood closely by him as he walked to take his turn by Bowman's side.

He was small in stature, thin and stooped from pain, but he attempted to put his arm around Bowman's shoulder. The gesture didn't work because Bowman was so much taller than him. Moved by the action, Bowman's eyes watered as he placed his arm gently around his father-in-law's scrawny shoulder.

"Ray, I am so sorry," he cried.

"Please, son, call me 'Dad,'" said the old man, burying his head in Bowman's chest.

Chapter 8

CLEANUP IN ROOM 117

Julie McKamey was jagged around the edges—an unrefined product of the Bear Wallow community of Caryville, Tennessee. She had five siblings, and four had different surnames than her; all were farmed out to relatives and acquaintances as the coexistence of her mother and boyfriend crumbled and fell apart, as it was sadly ordained. She was brought up by her mammaw in a shack that was transported down Caryville Mountain from an abandoned mining camp—a two-room abode that was positioned precariously on the edge of the creek bank. Every hard spring rain angered the creek, threatening the shanty with inundation. But every season offered a torrent of hardships that were weathered with all the dignity Julie and her grandmother could muster under the circumstances. As a child, her mammaw raised her at the foot of the cross, and Julie parlayed the lessons she learned at the Bear Wallow Holiness Church to heart; she had a good heart, tuned to love her neighbors and to champion the downtrodden, and she overlooked the fact that she was probably more oppressed than anyone she knew.

She was small for her age, and despite her fine-spun frame, challenged bullies who ridiculed those who were dressed poorly and suffered bullying with timidity.

"Hey, Margaret! What are you wearin' yore daddy's shoes fer?" sneered Harvey Bullock during recess.

"They ain't my daddy's shoes. They're my brother's shoes," said Margaret, the sleeves of her too large, holey sweater falling over her tiny hands.

"Looks like you're wearin' yore brother's sweater too," laughed Harvey, and his playground cohorts chortled at his cruel wit.

"Shut up, Harvey! Her brother's in Viet Nam now and if he was here, he'd kick yore behind into next week," yelled Julie Ann, standing protectively in front of Margaret.

"Well, he ain't here, so what are you goin' to do about it?" said Harvey, approaching her menacingly.

His group laughed hard as Julie put up her fists—a comical impression of John L. Sullivan.

Harvey pushed right through her guard, and smacked her hard.

None of the boys agreed with Harvey's actions, but they were afraid to challenge him. Ashamed of their cowardice, they dispersed quickly.

Harvey stood over her.

"You ain't got no brothers that I know of, so I'd jest learn to keep my mouth shut in the future, if I was you. The next time I'll use my fist," he said haughtily as he walked away.

Julie pinched her bleeding nostrils shut as Margaret helped her up. She reached into her crumpled lunch bag, grabbing a paper napkin that Mammaw had packed this morning, and dabbed at her nose.

"I'm sorry," said Margaret, staring sorrowfully at her defender.

"Don't you never mind," said Julie, taking the younger girl's hand.

"You hungry? Let's go over to that picnic table and I'll share my baloney sandwich with you."

Julie suffered more bloody noses, bumps, and bruises as time wore on, defending the browbeaten, taking the sides of those who were judged wrongly and overwhelmed by the odds against them. As she grew to womanhood, she had an unenviable track record of lost loves due to her dedication to the underdogs who were underdogs through their own volition. Now, unmarried and in her late thirties, she awoke every night wondering where the time went, and what she could have done to make her own life better.

She was polishing the floor at the end of the hall when the charge nurse interrupted her.

"Julie, we need a cleanup in 117, can you take care of it?"

"Sure. It ain't an overturned bedpan is it?"

"No. The patient has a bad arm and he knocked his food tray off the stand. I'd get it myself, but I have another patient that needs my help."

"That's okay. You don't get paid to do this stuff anyway," said Julie, not meaning to offend, just stating the facts in her straightforward way.

The room was dimly lit. The patient, Mr. Rafferty, lay in the bed, looking embarrassed and frustrated. He was the victim of a car wreck up on Massacre Mountain. She had noticed that the man rarely received any visitors, with the exception of the chaplain and members of the Kentucky State Police. At this juncture, she didn't realize that Bernard Rafferty was a pariah.

"There you go, buddy. That wasn't too big of a mess. Can I order you some more supper?" she said.

"Yeah. Do me a favor and mash some crushed glass up in it" came the bitter reply.

Julie stuck her mop in the bucket and rested the handle against the wall.

Her language had grown more colorful with age.

"What the hell kind of talk is that?"

"It's how I want to talk. What are you going to do about it?"

"Hey. I don't cotton to bully talk, never have. You ain't scarin' me, buster," she said as she started to roll her bucket out of the room.

"You ain't gonna tell on me, are you?"

"I ain't gonna tell on you if you tell me what's eatin' you," she said, her face softening.

Bernard rarely talked to anyone—but he sensed it was appropriate to confide in this woman.

"I just don't feel good. I'm sorry that I talked mean to you."

"That's okay, I have a feelin' that there's more on your mind that you're not tellin' me. Is everbody treatin' you okay?" she said, touching the edge of his pillow lightly.

"No worse than I deserve," he said.

"Well, I'm on the night shift for the next couple of weeks, and if you need anything, just yell. Sometimes the patient load gets heavy and the nurses are covered up. I can run errands for you if you'd like."

"What's your name?"

"Julie, and what's yours, honey?"

"Bernard."

"Okay, Bernard, you sleep tight. And don't be knockin' stuff over just to get me in here," she said.

"I will if I want to."

She thought she heard him chuckle, but couldn't be sure.

"Night, night, Bernard," she said as she gravitated to the hallway. She was met there by the charge nurse.

"Don't get too cozy with him. He's being evaluated, and the signs point to manic depression," she said, firing a stern look her way.

"Is he dangerous?"

"Could be. I would be too if I were responsible for the death of my loved ones," said the nurse.

"Was he drunk?"

"We're not allowed to divulge the blood-test results at this stage."

At that moment, the charge nurse was summoned over the tinny intercom. She turned and walked quickly down the hall toward the nurses' station.

As Julie returned to polishing the floor, it was her natural instinct to consider hoisting the banner in support of Bernard Rafferty.

It was an incremental process, but they became friends over the next few weeks as Bernard's substantial injuries healed. Bernard was initially spare with his words, but soon learned to carry on a decent conversation with chatty Julie.

"I suppose you know why I'm in here?" he said as she was dusting the corners of the room.

"Sure I know. You was in a car wreck," she said incredulously.

"You know what I mean…all of the details?"

She abandoned her dust mop and approached his bed.

"I've read some about it in the papers. Just tell me your side of the story, Bernard, if it will help," she said, berating herself for being disingenuous.

"My sister-in-law and nephew were killed on Massacre Mountain. I was driving. I wasn't drinking. I'll never forgive myself. I think I'm going crazy," he said, and Julie's tender heart broke as he fought to remain calm.

"God forgives you. I forgive you, if that means anything," she said, stroking his cheek with her palm.

"It means everything to me that you just touch me—nobody else will," he said, placing his hand on hers.

Julie liked the day shift. And she truly enjoyed his company as she polished the hallways.

"I believe this walkin' up and down the hall is helping me get my strength back. The doctor says I'll be gettin' out of here soon," he said.

"Well, I for one am goin' to miss you, Bernard. You've been great company," she said, as she arranged cleaning supplies on her cart.

He hung his head shyly and spoke in weak sentences.

"I was wonderin', if you're here on the day that I'm discharged, would you mind givin' me a ride home? I just live beyond the Gap in Harrogate. I'll pay you."

"You just let me know when and I'll give you a ride. I live close to the line in Middlesboro, anyway."

He chewed his nails.

"If the weather's bad, I'll find another way."

"Hell, I've drove that mountain in all kinds of weather."

"I know—but I don't want to lose… to cause you any trouble," he said as he hobbled back into his room.

Julie pondered why family members or friends hadn't volunteered to pick him up. A lump formed in her throat when she realized that he had no one.

When the day came of his discharge, he was nervous as a cat. He was sitting on the edge of his bed with his few belongings at his feet when she came in.

"Well, you ready to go, Bernard? My truck's all gassed up and ready to rumble over that mountain."

"Ready as I'll ever be," he said as an orderly helped him into the wheelchair.

She was a good driver, and she wasn't lying about knowing the mountain. Thankfully, the weather was nice, but she drove a little too fast to suit him. They drove through Harrogate, and he directed her to take a side road marked with a mailbox labeled "Rafferty." They drove for what seemed to be a mile up the long lane till they came to the house. She helped him carry his belongings up the porch steps, and was dismayed to see a note taped to the door, which was locked. Bernard read the message aloud:

> Bernard:
> I've taken the liberty to have most of your stuff delivered to your place over the shop. There are still a few things left here, but we'll get them moved eventually. Sorry you couldn't make it to Rosalee's and Durand's funerals. I'm sorry you couldn't make it to Mom's either. Hope you are healing well, both physically and spiritually.
> Bowman

Julie was mortified as Bernard paled and swayed.

"Here, honey, lean up against the porch railing. I'll take you to your apartment, it's on my way back home anyway," she said, furious at the cruelty she had just witnessed. She led him to the car, and returned to fetch his belongings.

"We'll have you home in no time. But first, let's stop at the grocery and get you some vittles—my treat," she said as they turned around in the yard.

She didn't expect much from Bernard's apartment, but was taken aback at the musty smell, mounds of clothing, and other articles that cluttered the living room, as if someone had flung open the door and tossed them in. Nothing had been touched since his departure over a month ago; his bed was unmade, and the aroma of something rotting drifted evilly from the refrigerator. On first inspection, it turned out to be a head of cabbage in the crisper.

"Why don't you get cleaned up, take your medicine, and I'll clean out this fridge before I stock it," she said.

"I can take care of that," he said, fumbling in his wallet.

"Here, let me pay you for all of this," he said, the bills quaking like aspen leaves in his trembling hand.

"Put that back in your wallet, and sit down. You look like hell," she said, removing some junk from the seat of a worn easy chair and giving him a gentle nudge in its direction.

He leaned his head back and closed his eyes, speaking weakly through a long, weary exhalation.

"I'm sorry, Julie. Why don't you go on home before it gets dark."

She didn't answer as she busily cleaned out the refrigerator and threw away the offending cabbage.

"I'll go home when I'm ready. Now get cleaned up and I'll fix us a sandwich," she said. She stayed the night, and eventually, for a long time after.

Bowman was scrubbing down the porch with a stiff-bristled broom and a bucket of soapy water when she arrived. She was surprised and pleased at his resemblance to his brother, except he had a full head of hair and a Kirk Douglas cleft in his chin. He paused in his work but didn't put the broom down, signaling that he didn't want to be disturbed.

"You Julie?"

"Right. And you cain't be nobody else but Bowman," she said as she climbed the steps and extended her hand amiably. He took it grudgingly.

"I guess you're here for the toolbox. I've got it right here," he said as he turned toward a glider at the end of the porch. She studied his mannerisms as he fetched the tools off the glider. He shuffled his feet when he walked as if he were exhausted. And his sad countenance rivaled his brother's constant expression.

"Well, thank you kindly," she said, hoping that he would ask about Bernard's recuperation. But that didn't happen. She gathered up all of her courage.

"May I call you 'Bowman'?"

"That's my name," he said, pouring a splash of soapy water on the porch.

"Bowman, why did you kick Bernard out of the house?"

He raised his voice, which was deep and tinged with bitterness. It frightened her, and she wasn't scared of much.

"Why? That apartment too small for your tastes?"

She glared at him.

"It wasn't his fault...the tests proved that he hadn't been drinking."

He started down the steps, and she flinched as she read the anger in his face.

"Do they have a test for being a damned moron?" he yelled, his face turning purple-red with rage.

She knew better than to push this man, and for once, kept her mouth shut. She could see that he was struggling to regain a semblance of calm, but was losing the battle.

"Bernard would have moved out anyway. He knew that the circumstances of my Rosalee's and Durand's deaths would preclude the two of us living under the same roof together. Don't worry, Julie, at my death, this house and this farm belongs to him—Rosalee and I saw to that a long time ago."

Julie was enraged at his words, especially his fancy professor-use of the word "preclude."

"All I know, Bowman, is what you wrote on that note taped to the door. And for your information, I ain't a damned bit concerned about movin' in to this place—now, or ever," she yelled as she threw the toolbox into the back of the truck, resulting in a lot of rattling and clanging.

He turned his back on her without a word and began scrubbing the porch again—a terse, wordless "good-bye" that could have also been construed as a "get the hell out of my sight" gesture.

Julie pealed out in a huge fan of gravel, and was happy to finally reach the main roadway.

"What a sad sonofabitch," she said as she pushed the truck in the direction of Harrogate.

Chapter 9

ROBERT BENTON, REDEEMER

Bowman was, indeed, sad as sad could be described. And deep down, he felt like a son-of-a-bitch for treating his brother like a nonentity; but that feeling was secondary compared to his sadness—an all-enveloping cloak of gloom that he had no intention of discarding as long as the visions of his sainted wife and son remained foremost in memory, and that would be forever. Although his mostly sleepless nights were fraught with painful dreams, he dreaded waking up to damnable reality each morning. He was unable to cope with the responsibilities of his work, and he groped his way clumsily through the university's labyrinth of hallways daily—a captive in a quagmire of melancholy. Both students and colleagues pitied this lost soul, and many were concerned about his sanity.

Dr. Robert Benton, president of the university, felt Bowman's pain. His wife and small daughter had been lost in a plane crash many years ago. And from that experience he knew that it would be wrong to say, "I know how you feel." He knew that nobody knows the intensity of your pain—and damn them for their stupidity, even if they believe they are sincere in their condolences. *This isn't a club*, he thought as some mourners moved through the line at the funerals, stating in reverent tones, and in various ways, "I know how you feel, buddy, I've been there."

Dr. Benton admired Bowman as much or more than anyone on his staff. Bowman had a fire in his belly for teaching and his knowledge, both scientific and homegrown, about agriculture was phenomenal. His rapport with students was magical; their devotion to him, and their excellent grades, were testament to that fact. Subsequent to the loss of Bowman's loved ones, Dr. Benton made some astute observations. Bowman reminded him of some hick, lost in a busy airport terminal. Everybody else knew where they were going: home to loved ones, greeting friends, getting on with business. Bowman was just "there"—a misfiring cylinder, coughing and sputtering, becoming still and useless in the machinery of life. Benton wasn't going to let that happen.

Bowman seated himself comfortably in the cushy cordovan leather club chair in Dr. Benton's office. Benton sat in the identical chair facing Bowman, after his secretary served them huge glasses of iced tea.

"It's sweet tea, just like you like it, Bowman," said Benton, cordially raising his glass in a toast.

"Here's to this year's graduating class, and to you, Bowman, for all of the young people you've inspired."

Bowman took a halfhearted sip out of his glass and set the sweating tumbler on a coaster on the side-table.

"Thank you, Robert. I have high hopes for all of them. I'll miss them."

Benton set his glass down and leaned forward, his hands in a prayerful clasp.

"What are your plans for this summer?"

"Just farming, that's all."

"Have you ever thought about taking a sabbatical? I know you've been under a lot of pressure."

"No."

Disappointed by the lackluster reply, Benton regrouped.

"Listen, I have a plan where someone can look after your crops, and you can help some people learn to grow sustainable crops and learn some new techniques at the same time. What do you say?"

Bowman took another sip of his tea and rose slowly from the chair.

"I appreciate your kindness, Robert. But I can look after my own crops, and I'm not up to hoeing anybody else's fields right now. But thank you anyway…"

Benton fumbled in his jacket pocket and extracted a brochure.

"Listen, I've already suggested that a group of undergraduates plant and harvest your fields as part of their upcoming grades and to help them get hands-on knowledge of the techniques that will be taught them in the future. And participation in this project will be of great importance—helping you in the future and perhaps, saving lives in the process. Besides, getting away from home sometimes can be healing. Absence makes the heart grow fonder, you know," he said, handing the brochure to Bowman, who studied the brochure briefly.

"W.A.S.? World Agricultural Society? I've heard of it, never was much interested in it," said Bowman, as he stuffed the brochure in his back pocket and started to leave.

Benton was a proud man, but his voice was pleading as he called after his friend.

"Please, Bowman. I don't want to say that I know how you feel, nobody does. But when my wife and daughter were killed, I took a sabbatical; was gone for almost three months to Central America. I learned so much about life and how blessed I was, despite my loss, that it turned my life around. Please, say you will think about it. I have the wheels set into motion to have you out of here within a week, if you'd like. As president of this university and your friend, I promise that I won't allow things on the home front to fail in your absence."

"I'll think about it, Robert," said Bowman, his stony expression belying his thoughts. As he closed the door behind him, Benton was discouraged.

Bowman sat at the kitchen table, drinking a beer for supper, and reading the brochure for dessert. His cat, Baby, sat in his lap as he read about faraway places that were described as much more exotic than what the pictures revealed: dusty, third-world destinations where rampant poverty and ignorance ruled, and desperation cried out from the soulful eyes of their hosts. His reservoir of sorrow was overflowing and he couldn't stand the thought of adding to it. He picked up the cat and strode over to the pantry for a can of food.

"My cup runneth over, Baby. Let's get you some food," he said as the cat drooled happily on his forearm. After she had consumed her supper, he opened the screen door.

"C'mon, Baby. I'm gonna lock you in the barn tonight. But there's plenty of trouble for you to find in there. Maybe you'll find a mouse or two for a midnight snack," he said as she followed him to the barn, prancing lightly at his feet.

Something found her attention immediately, and she climbed the ladder nimbly to the hayloft. Bowman backed the tractor out and closed the door quickly while she was distracted.

"I'll see you sometime in the future, Baby," he said as he climbed aboard the John Deere.

Exhausted by the formidable weight of sorrow, rather than walking Bowman rode the tractor to the gravesites. It was springtime, and the air was redolent with the fragrance of blooming trees, the grasses, wildflowers, and the freshly overturned earth waiting impatiently for planting. The chirping frogs rejoiced from the ponds and waterways as the tractor plodded over the soft earth. Formerly, the season of rebirth had been the favorite of Bowman's as he and Rosalee walked these fields, with Durand romping ahead of them. Now, all he could conjure up in his tortured mind were visions of death and dying. He couldn't help but think that this misery was karma in action, payback for the murder of that boy in the Ardennes. The sun was setting as he pulled up at the gate of the family burial ground. He labored to get down from the tractor and made his way slowly to the gravesites, which were overseen by a sour cherry tree in riotous bloom. Seating himself on the dewy grass between the graves, he pulled the pistol from his pocket—part of the ritual he'd performed many times, but never had the gumption to complete. He flinched as something soft brushed against his leg.

"Damn you, Baby! How did you get out of that barn?" he said as she jumped in his lap, reeking of Little Friskies cod and chicken livers, purring deeply. He scratched her head as he glanced at the gravestone to his left.

"Did you send her, Rosalee?" he said, somewhat relieved, but not cured.

Robert Benton was in deep thought, disturbed about the meeting that had transpired the day before, when there was a rap at his door. He was happy to see Bowman standing there, although Bowman's face registered neither delight nor sadness.

"Come in, Bowman, have a seat!" said Benton, leading Bowman with a royal sweep of his arm.

Bowman spoke first.

"Robert, I've thought long and hard about your offer."

Chapter 10

THE EXILES

Julie sifted through the stack of mail she'd withdrawn from the mailbox, and gasped as she came to the letter postmarked from Africa.

"Holy shit!" she screamed, hopped back into the car, and sped down the gravel road in a cloud of dust.

The letter was short and sweet—sweet because it was the only correspondence they had received from Bowman in nearly three months.

> Dear Bernard and Julie:
>
> It's getting close to the time when my work is finished here. If all goes right, I will be home in about five weeks. I've been sick for a while, and haven't achieved the goals I'd expected to achieve, but all in all, it's gone pretty well. I will keep you informed of my arrival date and time. Thanks for looking after the farm. I have much to tell you.
>
> Bowman

"I wonder what was wrong with him?" said Julie as she read over Bernard's shoulder.

"Most likely stomach problems. He started having them when he came home from the war," said Bernard as he folded the letter, stuffed it back in the envelope, and grinned satisfactorily.

"It's only a letter. But that's the most he's said to me since the... the accident," he said as she hugged him sweetly.

"I wonder what he has to tell us," she said.

"Probably to get the hell out of Tennessee," he said, and they both laughed at the dark humor. It was good to laugh, regardless.

Bernard and Julie had grown quite close, and had moved in together. Living in sin was not looked upon favorably by the churchgoing masses in East Tennessee, especially when Bernard was already considered an untouchable in large circles because of his role in the accident. For those reasons, their social life was minimal—almost nonexistent. On occasion, they would cross the Virginia line and visit a backwoods establishment called "The Grizzly Bar." It was not much: a few tables with mismatched chairs, a rough-hewn bar, pretty cold beer, and occasional booze from under the counter, including moonshine. It also featured a jukebox that blared lots of George Jones music, which they enjoyed. The Possum's cover of David Houston's "Almost Persuaded" was playing as they walked in and sat at the corner of the bar.

"What'll you'uns have? Beer? Beer? Or maybe beer?" said the large, bearded bartender jovially.

"I think we'll have beer, Bodie. The coldest you got," laughed Julie as Bernard held up two fingers and said, "Buds if you got 'em."

"I've got Buds and if we run out, there's plenty of PBR's left," said Bodie as he fished in the cooler.

"Save them PBR's for me," growled a stout fellow at the bar wearing a raggedy billed ball cap with the label "Garcia Fishing Tackle." His T-shirt, pocked with holes, was emblazoned with the image of a faded large-mouth bass on the front.

Bodie laughed as he sat the two beers down in front of Julie and Bernard.

"You've already put a dent in my stash, Harvey," he said, removing four dead soldiers from in front of the man.

"Fuck you," said Harvey.

"Watch your mouth," said Bernard, and Harvey started to get up off his bar stool. Bodie reached under the counter and retrieved a club.

"Don't make me use this, Harvey," he threatened, tapping the bat on the edge of the bar.

"Just get my beer, Bodie," ordered Harvey as he sat back down.

Julie was relieved, but wanted to distance herself from the idiot at the bar.

"Let's sit at a table, Bernard. I think I'd be more comfortable there," she said, eying the man warily. As they moved to the table, she searched her memory for where she had seen him before.

The evening wore on as Julie and Bernard depleted the small supply of Budweisers.

"We'll have two more for the road," said Bernard.

Bodie fished around in the cooler and shook his head.

"Sorry, Bernard, all we got left is PBR's."

"Then give us two PBR's then," said Julie.

"Comin' up, Julie."

Harvey, who was nodding, snapped back his head at her name.

"First of all, I said the PBR is mine. Second of all, that bitch at the table ain't getting' none of it," he slurred as he staggered off the bar stool.

Bodie secured the club again, as Bernard sprang from his seat at the table. Julie got up with him and spoke in his ear.

"Don't do anything, Bernard, remember your arm is still weak," she said, frantic.

Harvey was able to weave his way toward the table before Bodie got from behind the bar.

"Julie? You the same Julie from Bear Waller?" he mumbled.

She knew immediately who he was.

"That's right. And you're still that bully, Harvey Bullock," she said, recalling his voice and mannerisms. She continued, unable to keep her mouth shut.

"That was nearly thirty years ago. You sure hold a grudge, Harvey," she continued, holding Bernard back with both arms entangled in his.

"I smacked you that day. And I told you that if you ever fucked with me again, I'd use my fist," he said, balling up his big paw and advancing toward them. Bodie moved between them, club at the ready.

"You ain't gonna do nothin' but git outta here, Harvey, or I'll let you have it."

Harvey had the beer-fueled boldness to laugh in the face of the rock-hard hickory stick.

"Don't you know who this whore is? She hooked up with this piece of shit that killed his sister-in-law and nephew up on Massacre Mountain. Neither one of 'em is worth the powder to blow their brains out."

Bernard yelled and dove over the table, but Bodie beat him to the target, swinging away at Harvey's forehead.

Harvey crumpled to the floor like a house of cards.

Bodie fished in Harvey's boot and pulled out a Saturday night special. He jacked a round out of the chamber, and slid the Raven Arms .25-caliber semi-automatic into his hip pocket.

"I believe the stupid son-of-a-bitch would have used this. Two years ago, he shot Billy Marlow in the arm for accidentally taking a sip of his beer."

He picked Harvey up and headed for the door.

"Help me put him in the back of his truck. I can't call the sheriff, but I can stick him in there before he comes to," said Bodie, as Bernard helped him out the door with the tacky load.

Harvey was moaning as they dumped him in the truck bed.

"He don't live too far from here. If you'll foller me I'll drop him off at his place and you can bring me back," said Bodie as he slid into the driver's seat.

Bodie was right, Harvey lived no more than ten minutes from The Grizzly Bar, in a shack on the Kentucky line.

Bodie parked the truck in the gravel driveway, and trotted to Julie and Bernard's waiting truck.

"He'll be alright. He's got a thick skull. But I'll bet he sure has a headache when he wakes up," said Bodie as they sped back to the bar.

"We appreciate you," said Julie as they saw him to the door.

"It warn't your fault. This ain't the first time I've had to take him down a notch," he said, his eyes narrowing as he sized up Bernard.

"You really that boy who was in that wreck up on the mountain?"

"I'm afraid so," said Bernard.

Bodie shook his head sadly.

"I've owned this bar for nearly twenty years, and I'll bet that I've heard the stories of at least one hundred wrecks on that ridge. One of 'em involved my cousin. And I'll bet you a dollar to a dime that ninety-five percent of those wrecks was nobody's fault. They need to blast a hole through that mountain, and that'll stop the killin'," he said.

"I wasn't drinkin'," said Bernard, still lobbying for his innocence.

"That's why you ain't in jail, son. But I'm sure you're servin' time, in one way or another," said Bodie. "We'll be leaving now," said Julie.

"No offense, but don't come back, at least for a long time. There's too many assholes like that one we just left in that holler who come in here looking for a way to exact their pound of flesh, for one thing or another," he said, unlocking the door to The Grizzly Bar and disappearing into its dim environs.

She told him of the despicable slapdown that occurred nearly thirty years prior, and it infuriated him.

"That S.O.B. has never changed. You'd think that he would," said Bernard as they headed down the highway.

"Some people, even if they know they are doing wrong, remain the same for one reason or another," said Julie, and he thought painfully of his father.

"Have you ever been bullied, Bernard?"

"I think everybody is bullied at one time or another. I could always take care of myself. But there was one bully that I never could shake. What's worse is that I loved him," he said as he related the story.

Bernard was a gear-head from the get-go. He loved machinery of every kind, and he saved a lot of money, armed with an *International Harvester FarmAll Service* manual and a passion for tinkering, to keep their FarmAll 460 in good working order. He was responsible for keeping the machine properly lubricated, for adjusting the rear wheel tread, for attaching implements properly, and for myriad other mechanical duties that would have been costly and time consuming had he not applied his superb skills to the tasks. He loved what he was doing, but would have loved it a lot more had his father showed appreciation for his diligence.

He was mucking out a stall one afternoon when Jud came blowing through the barn door like a blustery wind.

"Well, you've done it now, boy!" he ranted.

Bernard leaned his rake against the wall, and walked tentatively towards his red-faced father.

"What's the matter, Daddy?"

"What's the matter, Daddy? What's the matter, Daddy?" mimicked Jud bitterly.

"The tractor is sittin' out in the north field, dead as a doornail. That's what's the matter!"

Bernard could not think of what could be wrong. He'd gone over the tractor with a fine-tooth comb the day before.

"Let me get my toolbox, Daddy, and I'll see if I can fix it," he said, heading toward the tool bench.

Jud stood in his way.

"No you won't, you idiot. Bowman and I will go to town and bring back Ralph Swanson from the dealer. He'll charge us twenty dollars an hour to fix whatever it is that you fucked up," screamed Jud as he backhanded Bernard.

Bernard flew backward, landing in the cow-dung pile in the stall. He tried to get up but Jud hit him again, this time with a closed fist.

"Get up, you little son-of-a-bitch! I'm goin' to take this out of your hide!" screamed Jud, and the terrified youngster refused.

"I said get up and take what's comin' to you!" he repeated, fists balled, neck veins bulging.

"Stay where you are, Bernard!" came a voice from the barn entrance.

Bowman, who was nearly five years older than Bernard at the time, big and strong for his age, came toward them.

"You stay out of this, Bowman."

"As much as I love you, I'd be wrong to do that, Daddy."

"Why's that? You have no authority here!" shouted Jud as he turned malevolently in the direction of his favored son.

"Yes I do, Daddy. I have the authority to stop anything that I see wrong. And I don't care what Bernard's done. You have no right to beat him like this; you have no right to disrespect him like this."

Jud acted as if he hadn't heard Bowman.

"Get up out of that cow shit, boy, and take your lickin' like a man."

"He's not a man yet. But I am, and I swear, I will fight you if you lay another hand on him," said Bowman, walking over to Bernard and extending a helping hand to him.

"If his mother ain't kissing his ass, you are. I don't think he'll ever be a man!" sneered Jud, as he stomped angrily out of the barn.

Ralph Swanson wondered how Bernard acquired a black eye and a swollen nose. But he kept his mouth shut as he examined the tractor.

"Your drive train's failed," said Swanson, wiping his hands on a rag. He noticed that Jud glared at his son.

"What would cause that? Have we not been maintaining it right?" said Jud, not taking his eyes off Bernard.

"Not really. The company has confessed that drive trains are failing after heavy usage, usually after about three hundred hours. They say that quality control has decreased because they are focusing on a lot of other products. The expense of fixing this will be mostly covered by the IH Company."

"How long will it take?"

"I really can't say; as you can imagine, there is a backup in repairing this equipment," said Ralph.

"Shit. Well, hop in the truck and we'll get the wheels set into motion," said Jud, shaking Ralph's hand.

"Hop in the back, boys, let's go to the house."

"We'll walk back," said Bowman, eyeing Jud spitefully as he draped his arm around the younger boy's shoulder.

"Suit yourselves," said Jud, and the son's animosity was palpable to Ralph.

Julie was deeply saddened by the story, and hated the man she'd never had the displeasure of meeting.

"It was a good thing Bowman was around then, wasn't it, honey?"

"Yes. I loved him, not realizin' that someday, he would hate me more than my father did," said Bernard, as they pulled into the drive.

Chapter 11

BUSTER AND THE BULLY

Harvey Bullock's daddy was a bully too, and taught Harvey well. He beat Harvey's mother, and he beat Harvey, with his fists and with his mouth, which was more hurtful and damaging in the long run than any physical beating could have ever been. He taught Harvey to hold a grudge against everyone for any perceived insult or slight, and that everyone, especially those smaller and weaker than him, was fair game for his rancor.

Harvey awoke this morning, cold and wet from the dew, not knowing how he got into the bed of his truck. His cap was lying beside him, and he placed it on his aching head. The bill of the cap fit crookedly, tilted by the monstrous lump on the corner of his forehead. The hat fell off as he pushed himself over the side of the truck and fell heavily in the driveway gravel. A shot of lightning pain flashed through his brain as he re-injured the lump. After a while, he managed the strength to raise himself up, and to stagger into the house. As he remembered the events of the previous evening, he reached into his boot to find that his pistol was gone. That was okay, he'd find it eventually; he had an arsenal of weapons stashed around the place. As his memory returned, so did his rage—especially his spite for that insulting bitch from Bear Wallow. Wobbly, he got up from the couch and went to the bedroom, where he rummaged around in his closet to find another weapon.

It was Saturday: Julie's day to clean and straighten up around the farmhouse. There really wasn't much to do since there was rarely anyone inside. But she dusted, and waxed, and watered the flowers on the porch to give some semblance of humanity to the place. It was also an opportunity for her to check their mail that was sent to the address.

"Come on, Little Buster, Etta, let's go home," she said to the Blue Heelers, son and daughter of the late family dogs Buster and Mary. They had been taken in to their care when Bowman went away. Bernard was working at the shop this Saturday, and she was eager to get to their apartment and cook their supper. Little Buster and Etta were already in the truck while she was locking up, and barked their orders to her to "get moving."

Harvey had no trouble finding out where they lived.

"I'm tryin' to find a girl named Julie and a man named Bernard. I owe them some money. Do you know where they live?" he asked the attendant at the Esso station in town, and the attendant gladly gave him the address of the Rafferty farm.

"I think Bernard is workin' at his shop today, but today is Julie's day to work at the farm. You'll be able to reach one or both of them, take your pick," he said, proving that everyone knows everyone's business in a small town.

"Thank ye," said Harvey, and he thought, *this is working out fine*, as he drove away in the direction of the farm.

The flag was down on the mailbox, signifying that the mail had run. Julie left the truck running as she got out to check the mail. She sighed as she fished through the stack of mostly advertisements and bills, when she heard the rumbling of a truck around the bend. She grinned, thinking that Bernard had gotten off work early and had driven out to join her. But it wasn't Bernard.

"Well, hidee, Miss Julie, remember me, Harvey?" he said, parking crossways in front of her, lumbering out of his truck and leaving the door open. She backed up and started to run for her truck.

"There, there, Miss Julie from Bear Waller. I just wanted to stop by and apologize fer the way I behaved the other night," he said, not a shred of sincerity in his voice.

Julie stopped to observe him. He was crazy-eyed, and the lump on his forehead elicited thoughts of Frankenstein.

"How'd you find out where I lived?" she said as she slid into the seat of her truck.

"They told me in town. Now you ain't agoin' nowhere; my truck's blockin' you and you got deep ditches on both sides of the road. Jest let me say I'm sorry, and I'll move along. I got a present for you and your old man," he said, as he reached into the cab of his truck and withdrew a shotgun.

Julie screamed, rolled her window up, and attempted to back up the lane, but ended up with one wheel in the shallow end of the ditch on the right side of the road.

"Now lookee what you done. I told you 'bout them ditches," he snickered as he stared menacingly at her from the roadbed. She said nothing as she hunkered against the passenger door.

""Don't bother tryin' to roll that winder up. I'm purty sure that this thang will take it out," he said, as he patted the barrel of the Mossberg.

"Don't, Harvey, don't," she pleaded.

He cocked the gun and pointed it at her.

"This may take two shots, but it will be all over in a flash," he chuckled. His chuckle turned to screams as Little Buster and Etta attacked him. He was no match for the dogs as they knocked him to the ground, snarling and ripping at his flesh. In the melee, the shotgun was flung into the ditch, where Julie retrieved it.

"Little Buster, Etta! Come here," she yelled, and they followed her command, tails wagging as if nothing had happened. Julie pointed the shotgun at Harvey, who was struggling to get to his feet.

"Now, git in that truck, and get your ass out of here before I blow you to Kingdom Come," she said as the dogs stared him down, low growls rattling in their throats.

Harvey was bleeding profusely from the neck and both arms.

"You might want to take yourself to the hospital, Harvey, you're lookin' pretty bad," she said, not taking her eyes or the barrel of the shotgun off of him.

He didn't answer, just groaned when he got into his truck, started it, and took off slowly down the road.

Julie rubbed the dogs' heads and patted their bodies vigorously.

"Come on, you two, let's see if we can get this truck out of the ditch," she said as her protectors frolicked around her.

Harvey was looking pretty bad by the time he arrived at his house. In the house he ripped a couple of old T-shirts up and wrapped them around his seeping wounds. He took a full pint of bourbon out of his kitchen cabinet, and drank half of the contents in a few swallows. Still furious, he made the trip to his bedroom closet and got his .357 off the top shelf. He went back to the kitchen and drank the rest of the bourbon, which soothed his physical pain—barely. He was having a difficult time putting his thoughts together for a plan of action when he heard sirens echoing through the hollow. Suddenly, he made a decision. As the sheriff's cruisers came to rocking halts in his driveway, they were greeted by a loud blast and a strobe flash of light from inside the home.

Julie and Bernard were disturbed that Harvey had committed suicide, even though he was a threat to their lives.

"I'm glad he's gone. But I can't stop thinkin' what a miserable S.O.B. he was," said Bernard as they lay in bed together.

"If I remember correctly, his daddy was said to have been just like him: crazy as an outhouse rat," said Julie, as she lay her *Family Circle Magazine* down on the nightstand.

"If you're ready to go to sleep, so am I," she said, turning off the lamp.

She built what he called her "fort," lining pillows along her side so she could switch a sleep-warmed pillow for a cool one, when she experienced a hot flash. That project completed, she scooted over next to Bernard, placing her head on his shoulder.

"You think you're going to sleep good tonight, honey?"

"You never know. I get to thinkin' about stuff, and I can't shut my mind down," he answered. They were quiet for a while, falling in step with the rhythm of each other's breathing, when she spoke.

"You know, Bernard, I'm glad you didn't turn out like your daddy."

"Probably 'cause I'm a chicken," he said as he patted her shoulder.

"I think you're courageous," she said, pecked him on the cheek, and rolled over.

He thought about her comment for a while. And based on her soothing words, he slept well that night.

BOOK 3
ANTWERP

Chapter 12

MADAME de CROY'S BOSOM

The setting winter sun reflected mauve and pink off the waters of the river Scheldt as it wound its way west to the North Sea. Dr. Christophe Peeters stood at the window in his office in the neighborhood of Linkeroever, admiring the scene—the first time he had relaxed since he began work at 6:30 this morning. His practice was fabulously successful; first, because he was a top-quality physician with a sterling resume; secondly, because his patients, mostly residents of the beleaguered city of Antwerp, had been denied quality medical attention during the years the war dragged on. Like their city, which was rebounding quickly from the German occupation, shoveling its way from beneath the detritus of war, the residents focused on overlooked health problems, in preparation for a revitalized future. Their lines at medical facilities were endless; and so were responses to their demands.

Christophe's brain and body were buzzing from the activity of the day; decisions to be made regarding the human condition; pronouncements informing patients of impending death, bright or fragile futures, business decisions, and other decisions involving his personal life—which was a miniscule piece of the pie, but nonetheless, not to be overlooked in the midst of the chaos of attending to others.

He turned out the lights, lit a cigarette, and watched as a gaily lit barge cut cleanly through the pink and gray, glassine surface of the water, and he remembered when there was no traffic allowed on the river until all mines left by the Germans in their hasty departure had been cleared. There was a soft tap at the door.

"Come in," he said, just above a whisper.

"Everyone is gone. Everything is locked," she said in a hoarse, lusty murmur, stepping out of her lab coat and undergarments as she crossed the room to him. She was completely naked when she reached him, where he sat on the corner of his desk. He swallowed hard at her beauty, and touched her exquisite breasts lightly. She shivered.

"You must be cold," he said, as he unbuttoned his shirt.

"Actually, I'm very hot," she answered huskily, clearing the desk-top off with a sweep of her hand, reclining in a tempting pose on the surface.

"Come, Doctor, and examine me."

He gladly accepted her invitation.

Catrin de Jonge Peeters gazed critically at herself in the full-length mirror. She was still petite and her breasts were pert; her hair was glossy, her lips full, and her eyes, liquid brown, long-lashed, and al-mond shaped, resembled the eyes of a doe. She had gained a little weight around the hips and buttocks since the war ended. But, that was good; as a member of the peripatetic resistance, she was on the move con-stantly, teetering on the verge of gaunt, as were many of her comrades. One of those comrades was her lover. Now he was her adored husband and a successful physician in private practice in Antwerp. She continued her career as an epidemiologist at St. Elizabeth's Hospital, where she'd first met Christophe during their internships. She fled with him dur-ing the German occupation to join the Comet Line Resistance Group in Brussels. There, they helped Allied soldiers and airmen return to Britain. Sometimes, it seemed that they had more time together in war than they did these days. But the current time was used simply and wisely: shopping at the Grote Market; touring the medieval castles; cy-cling through the Antwerpse Kempen, through forests and along canals and meadows; eating out at a fashionable restaurant on occasion. She mostly enjoyed lengthy summer vacations at his boyhood home near St.

Vith, in the Ardennes Forest; his relatives were sturdy peasant stock who doted on her, making her feel like nobility and family at the same time. She cried as they cried over the tragic memory of Christophe's sainted brother Armandus' death, and the boy's benediction on the man who killed him; she sobbed when Christophe knelt at the graves of his loved ones when they visited the cemetery in the forest; she felt a deep kinship with them, and hoped to share these precious moments with her and Christophe's children in the future.

Her heart leaped as she heard his key click in the tumbler. Throwing on her robe, she took the steps two at a time to greet him at the landing.

"For you, my lady," he said, handing her the bunch of white tulips. Moved to tears, she responded, throwing one arm around his neck.

"Je t'adore," she whispered in his ear.

He laughed.

"I adore you too, what smells so good?"

"Before I tell you, what smells so good on your neck? Is that perfume?" said Catrin, a pout forming on her rosebud lips.

"Indeed it is. Old Madame de Croy squeezed my face long and hard between her huge breasts when I told her that her blood pressure had reached the safety level," he laughed, and relieved, Catrin laughed too.

"Then I will tell you what smells so good. Beef stew in beer, your favorite. And to celebrate Madame de Croy's health, I bought a bottle of delicious Belgian Pinot Noir," she said, wielding the corkscrew expertly, pouring hefty portions into each of their glasses.

The meal was delicious, and the wine flowed freely as they laughed and discussed their workdays. He helped her clean the table and stack the dishes. Afterward, a little bit tipsy, Catrin molded herself against him.

"J'ai besoin de toi…I need you," she said seductively, closing her eyes and snuggling against his neck.

"I feel the same way, but I can't guarantee a great performance, I am so tired and a little bit drunk. You turn the bed down while I take a shower, and let's see what happens," he said, kissing her hard on the mouth.

"Agreed! I'll meet you in the boudoir," she replied, as she hurried toward their bedroom.

The shower felt good, and Christophe scrubbed himself well just in case "Madame de Croy" had accidentally left some of her bouquet lingering about his private areas.

Amelie Dubois looked ravishing in a festive sheath dress that accentuated her lovely figure. It was Christmastime in Antwerp, and as office manager of the group of six physicians, she was hostess of their annual holiday party.

"Vrolijk Kersfeest, Dr. Peeters and Madame Dr. Peeters, welcome to the celebration," she said, handing Christophe a full champagne flute.

"May I get you something to drink, Madame Peeters? I know that you are not partaking of alcohol since you are due any time now," she said while concentrating her smoky gaze on Christophe.

Catrin, eight months pregnant and feeling dowdy, was intimidated by this confident, beautiful creature who paid too much attention to her husband.

"No, not right now. I'll get something later," Catrin said, and was embarrassed as in a motherly fashion, Amelie picked a piece of lint from Christophe's jacket shoulder.

"Well then, enjoy yourselves. Dr. Peeters, since I am unaccompanied this evening, may I have the pleasure of a dance when the orchestra plays?"

"As long as it's to the tune of a slow song," he said, as she kissed him on both cheeks.

"It was nice seeing you again, Madame Peeters," said Amelie, as she bussed Catrin's cheek and walked quickly away to greet other arrivals.

Catrin's dark eyes flashed as Christophe escorted her to their assigned table.

"It seems that Miss Dubois wears the same perfume as old Madame de Croy," she whispered sardonically to her husband.

The evening was tortuously long for Catrin; agonizing for Christophe.

Catrin was coldly silent as they drove home from the party.

Christophe was tentative in response to her rebuffs.

"Aren't you feeling well, darling?" he said, reaching over to pat her shoulder.

"No!" she cried. "My heart is broken!"

"What are you talking about…?"

"I saw the way she plastered her hips against your body and held the back of your neck while you were dancing. I watched as the other wives stared and whispered amongst themselves. You cannot tell me that you and that bitch haven't been having an affair," she screamed, voice cracking, tears flowing freely.

He attempted to assuage her outburst with a desperately contrived lie.

"Catrin, she is just…"

"Turn here."

"Why here?"

"To St. Elizabeth's. My water has broken," she stated matter-of-factly.

The birth of the perfect baby girl did little to lessen Catrin's fury or Christophe's angst.

She cuddled the child to her breast as he hovered over them.

"Well, are we going to name her Camille, or Margot?" he said, pleasantly as possible.

"'Camille' was your choice, wasn't it?" she said in a weak, feathery-around-the-edges voice, sapped from the ordeal of birth.

"Yes," he replied as he reached to touch his daughter's warm and nearly hairless head.

Catrin turned her shoulder and shielded the child away from his touch.

"Then we will name her Margot," she said, her voice becoming stronger as the full brunt of her anger returned.

"You can save the name 'Camille' for any children you may father with that whore you have been screwing," she spat.

The attending nurse took Christophe's elbow.

"I am sure you wouldn't mind leaving now, Dr. Peeters, so your wife and baby can get some rest," she said, escorting him to the door.

He didn't have the gumption or the energy to object to her temerity.

Christophe was basically a good man. But he was just a man, subject to the many temptations offered to a person of his stature, particularly the temptations offered by the intensely lovely Amelie Dubois—a woman possessing the libido of a rabbit.

"We must put an end to this. Catrin is not alone in her suspicions; everybody knows," he lamented to her in his darkened office one evening. She came to him as she donned her clothing.

"Please let me comfort you," she said, drawing his head to her breast. She kissed his neck and massaged his shoulders. After a while, he responded hotly to her touch and they made love roughly. As they lay in each other's arms, panting from their most recent erotic endeavor, she spoke first.

"I must admit that I am addicted to you. If we're going to break this thing off, let's do it in increments. Besides, there is no reason why a man can't have his cake and eat it too," she said, rolling over on top of him as they undressed each other again. She smiled slyly in the dark, knowing that their steamy liaison would never end as long as she had control over his body and soul.

Catrin and Christophe's love blossomed during the war, the danger, the excitement, and the commitment to saving others fueling their devotion to and passion for one another. They were confident that they would be together forever, love-struck egos dismissing any shred of a thought that forgiveness was an essential element in the recipe for longevity in a marriage or relationship. Christophe knew now the need of forgiveness for his infidelity, and he would have begged for forgiveness if not for his pride and his addiction to Amelie—the thorn in his paw that festered, putrefying, spreading its poison throughout his life.

The thin thread that held together their precarious marriage now was little Margot—the joy, the reason for their lives. She kept the fire of love tended in Catrin's heart, and ignited a flicker of optimism for Christophe that one day he would receive pardon for his sins. Despite his expectations, he foolishly continued his affair with Amelie, but hoped to end it soon.

Catrin was diapering Margot when the phone rang.
"Hello? Yes, this is Doctor Peeters, what can I do for you?"
An obviously disguised female voice spoke to her.
"Doctor Peeters, your husband is meeting with that bitch in his

office as we speak. There is a key beneath the mat," said the owner of the voice, and the phone was hung up immediately.

Catrin, crazed with anger, called her neighbor, a widow, who lived next door.

"Mrs. Van de Velde, this is Mrs. Peeters. I have an urgent errand to run, do you have a moment to look after Margot? Good. If you could come over immediately, I will appreciate it," she said. When she hung up the phone, she raced to the closet and took a box from the top shelf.

They made love for a long time. And when they were finished, he put his clothes back on. She remained naked, in hopes that they would rekindle their lovemaking one more time after this tawdry respite. He lit cigarettes for both of them.

"Amelie, as I said before, we can't go on like this. Please, I ask that you let me go," he said, taking her hand tenderly in his.

She smiled seductively as she moved toward him.

"What's the matter? Are you losing your taste for cake? I'm not," she said, kneeling before him.

The sound of a closing door clicked in the outer office.

"I thought you said you locked up?" he whispered as she sprang to her feet.

Before she could answer, there was a rapping at his office door. Amelie ran to a darkened corner of the room as he answered the knock.

"Yes, who is it?"

Another hard rap. He moved closer to the door.

"Who is it?"

A key was inserted in the lock and the door flew open.

"Catrin, I was just closing up. What are you doing here?" he said, his nervousness betraying his lie.

Catrin failed to answer as she flipped on the overhead lights. Amelie screamed as she cowered, naked in the corner.

Catrin reached into her trench-coat pocket and extracted the Luger.

"Remember this, Christophe? It was captured from a German officer, and you gave it to me," she said, pointing the pistol and him, then, at Amelie.

"Please, allow me to put my clothing on," pleaded Amelie, not moving from her position in the corner.

Catrin laughed.

"No. I want them to find you just like you are, and what you are: a conniving whore. So don't move, as I deal with this adulterous bastard."

Christophe held his hands out in front of him as she moved closer.

"Your hands are not enough to stop these bullets," she said. Amelie screamed and fainted as Catrin calmly pulled the trigger.

Christophe collapsed, and moments later, his head appeared comically above his desk as Catrin spoke in a calm voice.

"Unfortunately, I misplaced the ammunition some time ago. I am going home to my Margot, and to pack your things. You might want to attend to that slut. I believe she has pissed on your carpet," said Catrin, as she closed the door behind her.

Amelie tendered her resignation by phone the next day.

Christophe was relieved that she didn't want a divorce. "Too messy," she said. But she moved out of the apartment quickly and efficiently, lock, stock, and baby, despite his begging and pledges to be faithful. He adored little Margot, and was pleased that Catrin allowed him time with her. As Margot got older, her mother allowed her to spend quality time with her cousins in the Ardennes, and Catrin stayed there periodically, but only without his presence. She had no family, and his family loved her and worshipped Margot regardless of Catrin and Christophe's troubles. Catrin immersed herself in her work, writing important papers on the causes of effects of health and disease conditions, taught at the university, and was well respected in the public health arena.

Christophe and Catrin were both beautiful people, considered "a catch" by their friends, acquaintances, and by those who admired them from afar. As it was with most separations, sides were taken and alliances were formed, and since they still remained married, neither was approached by would-be paramours—at first.

Christophe, like many European men, was blasé about marital indiscretions, and he and his colleagues shared the philosophy that it was morally acceptable if "you knew how to do the wrong thing the right way." But his adherence to that philosophy was severed when he lost Catrin and Margot, whom he realized were the loves of his life. For a long while, outside of his professional life, he lived a monkish existence, wearing the hair shirt of celibacy as penance for his infidelity. Unfortunately, it didn't take long for him to succumb to the wiles of a designing woman.

Sylvain, a nurse who worked for Christophe and his colleagues, had her eyes on Christophe even before Amelie sunk her hooks into him. It was she who had called Catrin and alerted her to their affair in the office that night. Now that Amelie was out of the picture, the odds were in Sylvain's favor, and she planned to use them to her advantage.

She was comely and she knew it, with a body that made her nurse's uniform look like an evening gown.

"Dr. Peeters, a few of us from the office are going to dinner at Ciro's this evening; would you like to go along?" she said as she handed him a patient's chart.

Christophe had once been a social person, and missed the

opportunity to go out with friends. He decided to end the fast.

"Sure, we...I mean I used to dine there often and enjoy their steaks. What time?"

"Nine o'clock. I have a table reserved," said Sylvain, ecstatic that her plan was working.

As usual, he arrived late. The maitre d' recognized him, addressed him by name, and led him to the table.

"Good evening, Dr. Peeters," said Sylvain, who was dressed in a sleek, chic dress, looking fabulous.

"Where is everyone?" he asked as he was seated at the table for two.

She looked sad and angry.

"One by one, they cancelled out," she said, not naming the names of the invitees. "I think it's this damned flu that's going around," she said, as the waiter brought the wine list.

He realized the ruse at once, and excused himself.

"Where are you going?" she demanded.

"I'm sorry, I think I have the flu," he said, and made his way to the coat check station. He was not about to spoil any chance of reunification with Catrin.

"Will the gentleman return, madame?" said the wine steward.

Sylvain didn't answer his question, but issued a demand instead.

"Clear his napkin and dinnerware from the table and take his glass."

"My pleasure. Have you decided on the wine?"

"I'll have the Cabernet Franc."

"Excellent choice," said the waiter as he left the table.

He returned with a bottle of the cab, showed her the label, and poured a bit for tasting.

"To your liking?" he said.

"Fine. Fill the glass," she said bitchily.

He followed her instruction and started to leave.

"Leave the bottle," she fairly shouted. She downed the first glass of wine and poured herself a second. As she fumed, she pondered calling his spouse with an update of his faux shenanigans.

Chapter 13

THE UNCONVENTIONAL FAMILY

As the years passed, Catrin received calls from numerous women who'd attempted to cajole Christophe, but failed; and was apprised of false sightings of him in the company of other women. Despite those impediments to their relationship, she gradually became cordial with Christophe, and on occasion, she would agree to meet with him and take Margot to the zoo, the park, to a museum, or to visit their getaway apartment in the fishing village of Volendam, near Amsterdam, where they would spend the day sailing along the canals. Christophe, who had become wealthy with his growing practice, drew from his well of courage and asked Catrin often to reunite with him, but the answer was always an emphatic "no" and she would turn to ice for the remainder of their visit. They both shared immense pride in Margot. She was an excellent student, and was interested in everything, her intelligence being well-noted. She was tall, like Christophe and shared his strong chin and jawline. Her eyes were almond-shaped, her hair glossy auburn, and her lips formed a cupid's bow—all gifts from her mother. Margot seemed happy with their arrangement, but that was all she'd ever known. She knew that she was loved, and that was the most important thing.

"What time will you pick me up tomorrow, Mamma?" said Margot, as her mother retrieved her overnight case from the trunk of the car.

"Your father and I have discussed that. About ten o'clock, if that's okay with you. Your birthday party is scheduled for two o'clock, and

I'd like to get you home in time for that. You have a good time at the restaurant this evening, and don't eat too much," said Catrin, kissing her daughter on both cheeks.

"I will, Mamma. Thanks for the ride."

Margot had a key to her father's lavish apartment, and let herself in. As she busied herself getting ready for her twelfth birthday celebration this evening, the phone rang, and she hurried to answer it.

"Hello, darling. Just called to say that I am sorry not to be there, but I promise to arrive in time to take you to supper, okay?"

"Sure, Pappa, it takes me a long time to get ready anyway."

"Just like your mother," he laughed and hung up.

The past decade had been kind to Amelie. She had retained her beauty, but was not blessed with marriage to a physician, which she had hoped for. She did sate her matrimonial desire by hooking up with a dentist who was very successful. She managed his practice and they closed up for three months in the summer and fled to Aruba for a long holiday. He was older than her by twenty years, and she eyed the young men who worked at the resort lasciviously when he wasn't around. Back home, she had planned trysts with several men that turned out to be modestly successful, but none of them could compare with her long-ago, heated liaisons with Christophe Peeters. She saw him on the street recently, and visions of those steamy sessions fired her libido. Everyone knew that he was still married, although he didn't live with his wife. She smiled as she pulled up in front of his apartment, satisfied that she was the reason for their separation. It was a gamble, but she hoped to catch him at home this Saturday morning.

Margot raced to answer the door chime, thinking that her father had managed to get away early. She was disappointed to see the visitor, but not as disappointed as the visitor was to see her.

"Uh, hello. Is Doctor Peeters home?" said the attractive woman.

"No, but he will be back in a few hours. Would you like to come in?"

Amelie, curiosity aroused, accepted her invitation. Margot led her to the couch and invited her to sit down.

"My name is Margot, I'm his daughter," she said proudly.

No doubt. You look just like him and that bitch, thought Amelie as she smiled pleasantly at the girl.

"You're a beautiful little girl. How old are you?"

"I'll be twelve on Sunday, but Pappa is taking me out tonight because he can't make my birthday party tomorrow. What's your name?"

"How rude of me. My name is Amelie. I used to work with your father and I was in the neighborhood. Since it's Saturday, I thought I would find him at home."

"He works all of the time," said Margot.

"I know. When I worked for him, we spent a lot of overtime in the office," said Amelie, savoring those moments in her mind.

"Would you like a cookie?"

"No thank you. I have to be going, but I will drop in some other time," said Amelie, as she rose from the couch to go.

"I'll tell Pappa that you were here."

"No, no. Please don't tell him, I'd like to surprise him sometime; promise not to tell?" said Amelie, patting her shoulder.

"I promise. Thank you for coming by," said Margot politely

Amelie was disappointed that Christophe wasn't there, but had not given up on her plan.

I'll stop by to see him at eleven o'clock on a Sunday night if I have to, she thought as she started her car.

Catrin was in high spirits as she drove to pick Margot up on Sunday morning. Margot had called early to tell her about the fantastic evening her father had planned for them. He had asked Catrin to come along, but she had refused. Now she wished she hadn't.

"He gave me a corsage. And a violinist came to our table and played 'Happy Birthday.' Then, Pappa gave me a sip of his wine," Margot babbled excitedly.

Catrin was warmed by the love of Christophe for his daughter and her thoughts nearly centered on the aspect of returning to him, to provide a more normal life for the precious child they had made together.

They were waiting curbside for her when Catrin arrived.

"I thought we'd wait out here for you, knowing that you have a lot to do for the party today," said Christophe.

"When do you leave for Paris?" said Catrin, bending her head to speak to him through the passenger's window.

"Tomorrow afternoon; I'll be gone for a week," he answered.

"Maybe we can get together soon afterward," she said, smiling earnestly.

He looked mildly shocked and pleased.

"You can count on it," he said as he kissed Margot on the head.

The party was in full swing, and with Catrin's precise planning, was pretty much taking care of itself. Catrin took a breather and poured herself another glass of wine. She went into the kitchen to drink it, basically because Margot nagged her for imbibing too much. As Margot became older, learning to care for herself, Catrin did drink on more than an occasion—a reward for her hard work, and relaxing without the company of a man. She poured herself another glass as people were leaving.

"Mamma, thank you for a great party! I wish Pappa could have been here!" said Margot as she helped with the dishes.

"Me too. I'm sure he would have enjoyed your friends. But, as you know, business takes precedence with him; my business takes a lot of my time too," she said, draining her glass of cabernet.

"When did he say he would be back, Mamma?"

"He'll be gone for a week."

"That's too bad. A friend of his is looking for him, and she stopped by his apartment the day you dropped me off. She said she used to work for him—a very pretty lady."

Catrin blanched.

"Did she mention her name?"

"It was Amelie, I believe…," said Margot, who was interrupted by the ringing of the phone.

"I'll get it!" she said as she ran to the living room.

Catrin fumed as she poured another glass of wine, and grimaced as she heard Margot say, "Hello, Pappa!"

"Let me speak to him when you're finished, please, Margot. I'll be on the extension in the bedroom," she said as she made her way to the bedroom, wineglass in hand.

When she was sure Margot was off the line, she spoke to him.

"How's your meeting going, Christophe?"

"Well, it's not started yet, I'm taking a break from writing a speech I'm supposed to deliver at the general session tomorrow. How did the party go?"

She ignored his remark.

"Why don't you tell me the truth, you philandering son-of-a-bitch? She's there with you now, isn't she?"

Flabbergasted, Christophe failed to answer.

"She is, isn't she?"

"Who, who are you talking about?" he stuttered.

"Amelie! Amelie! You know, the bitch that pissed on your carpet. That slut that you were planning on screwing while our daughter was in your apartment!"

Angered at her slurry outburst, not knowing if his daughter was in hearing distance or not, he parried her wrath.

"Shut up, Catrin. There's nobody here with me. You're drunk, and why should you care about my needs? We haven't had relations in over a decade, despite the fact that I have begged you to come back to me. Besides, I know that you have been with men, and I am not going to live the life of a monk just because you are a bitch!" he yelled, his voice escalating with his increasing ire.

She slammed the phone in the cradle.

"Son of a bitch!" she snarled, then caught her breath as she noticed Margot standing in the doorway.

The traffic was erratic as Catrin drove Margot to the Academy the next morning.

"Damned Vespas," shouted Catrin, blaring her horn at another operator of a pesky scooter who darted in front of her car. She pounded the steering wheel in cadence with the pounding in her skull, as Margot peered ahead sullenly.

"Is it too early for you to have a glass of wine, Mamma? That might settle you down," she said out of the corner of her mouth.

"You listen to me, young lady. Just because you're twelve years old doesn't give you the authority to talk to your mother like that!" said Catrin, switching the music off the radio and pulling up to the curb.

Margot flung open the door, slid out of her seat, and slammed the door so hard the car rocked.

"And just because you're my mother does not give you the right to call my father a son-of-a-bitch," she snarled as she walked briskly away.

After watching Margot meet with some friends and walk into the school building, Catrin held her face in her hands, wishing she were somewhere, anywhere but at this time and place. She slammed the steering wheel again with the palm of her hand.

"I almost gave in! I almost forgave that son-of-a-bitch!" she said aloud, thinking that it would be good to get far away from him, if only for a little while, to steel her resolve to make him a nonentity in her life.

Catrin's boozy phone call flustered Christophe, but he held himself together to deliver an excellent speech at the meeting the next day; it was received well by his colleagues, who lauded him and praised his eloquent presentation. He was less than triumphant at the airport the next morning, weighed down with angst over Catrin's boozy offensive on the phone, and he felt terrible after calling Margot, who tearfully confessed that she had met with Amelie. As his plane took off from Orly, all other emotions were put aside as he was consumed with rage over the conniving Amelie, who seemed bent on destroying his relationship with Catrin. *I will put an end to you, one way or another*, he thought, wondering if he was doomed ever to make things right with Catrin.

The receptionist was intrigued by the good-looking, solemn-faced man who strode with great purpose up to the counter.

"May I help you?" she asked.

"I'd like to speak to your business manager, and also her husband. I'd like to speak to them now," he demanded, his fist striking the counter solidly. Noticing his anger, other patients put their magazines down to observe the scene.

"Dr. Vandermeer is with a patient right now. Do you have an appointment with Madame Dubois?" she said icily.

"No. She tried to make an appointment with me. Now will you

direct me to her office, or his?" said Christophe, in a more than menacing tone that was rising as the moment continued.

"What's going on here?" snapped Amelie, then she smiled nervously as she spied Christophe at the window.

"Christophe! To what do I owe this pleasure?" she said as she sashayed toward the window, hand extended in a professional manner of greeting. He ignored the gesture.

"This visit is not for pleasure. My daughter told me about your visit. I am here to tell you to stay away from me…stay away from my daughter. I feel nothing for you…I retract that statement, I feel a great deal of animosity for you, and you would be wise to STAY AWAY FROM ME!" he shouted as he stormed out of the office.

"You bastard!" Amelie said under her breath.

"What's this all about?" said her husband, who stood in the door, still wearing his protective mask.

"Nothing. Nothing," replied Amelie, as visions of extended Aruba vacations dissolved in her head.

BOOK 4
CONGO

Chapter 14

INTO AFRICA

For Catrin, life had become quite humdrum, with endless papers to write, boring meetings, and redundant teaching assignments. Margot was growing rapidly now, and did not need the motherly attention she'd demanded as a child. She had her friends, studies, and a wide world of interesting things to explore, with minimal chaperoning required. In Catrin's mind, the only person in the family in need of a chaperone was Christophe, and she was eager to distance herself from him. For these reasons, she jumped at the offer from the World Health Organization to research some major infectious diseases that were prominent in the Congo.

"The job will last about three to four months. And you will be required to study food- and water-borne diseases, hepatitis A and B, typhoid fever, vector-borne diseases like malaria and dengue fever, and, of course, hemorrhagic fever. There have been great strides in treating these diseases of late, but we need more articulate reporting than what has been done. You will be working with top professionals, such as yourself, from all over the world," said Father Van Roey, hospital administrator for St. Elizabeth's Hospital. "And you'll be pleased to know that there is a leper colony close by where you'll be working; it is in great need of your expertise," said Sister Marie De Smet, a nurse and representative of the Missionaries of the Sacred Heart.

Catrin flew from Antwerp to Paris, to London, and finally embarked on the final leg of the trip to the Congo. A representative from the village was unable to meet her at the derelict airport, but she was assured that a driver of a Land Rover would meet her at her hotel. Unfortunately, she had to stay in Leopoldville overnight, before the Land Rover and driver would arrive.

The airport in Leopoldville was a slum in itself: torn carpets, cracked floors, rain-stained ceiling tiles, bloated and sagging, appearing ready to drop. The aroma of starchy food permeated the place, and solemn-faced soldiers lined the corridors along with food and trinket vendors, plenty of shoe-shine men, whose customers were mostly miserable-looking white men, neckties askew, half-moon-shaped sweat stains in the armpits of their suit jackets. The scenario outside of the airport was worse: a sea of humanity sweating beneath the torturous African sun, screaming, pushing, shoving, hawking everything imaginable.

"You are wanting a ride, madame?" said the thin ebony-black man wearing the soiled dashiki.

"Yes, actually, I do need a ride," said Catrin as she sweltered at curbside.

"Then step into my automobile and I will take you wherever it is that you would like to go," he said, attempting to grab her baggage, but she stopped him.

"I can handle my own baggage. Where is your car?" she said, standing in front of her gear.

He laughed, and pointed across the boulevard which was jammed with all manner of traffic, including mules and donkey-driven carts.

"See that yellow Citroën? That is my car. Where is your destination?"

"The Royal Leopoldville," she said, wiping her face with her hand.

"Ah yes, I know the location well, on the outskirts of town. It will cost you a little over fifty francs."

"I can give you that."

"Plus tip?" said the driver.

"Yes, plus tip," she said brusquely.

He held up a finger and amidst blaring horns and cursing, made his way across the boulevard to his automobile. He disappeared for a while, and she was beginning to think that he would never return when he blared his own horn and pried his way to curbside.

"May I help you with your luggage now, or would you rather load it into the boot yourself?" he said with a smirk. She performed the duty herself.

The Citroën, a ten-year-old DS 19 model, had seen its better days; dented, pocked, and rusted with a wired-on front bumper, rattling and coughing—a faded yellow cigar-shaped vehicle that Europeans would regard as comical in appearance, but it fit in perfectly with the mosaic of decrepit transportation available in Leopoldville.

The interior reeked, and Catrin gagged as she slid in to the backseat, which was stained with a sizeable hole in the middle.

"What is that smell?" she said of the aroma of sour milk and urine that permeated the interior.

"People here have a tendency to leak," he laughed, then blew his horn and cursed the driver in front of him .

"Ah, Nino Malepet!" said the driver as he turned the volume high on the radio.

The music sounded like rumba, but with more frantic percussion—made worse by the tinny speakers in the dashboard.

"Will you shut that off!?" yelled Catrin above the cacophony. The driver was offended, offering a sarcastic reply.

"What? You do not like soukous music? I should have known that it would not be appreciated by a person like you."

"What do you mean by that?"

He ignored her and asked where she was from.

"Antwerp."

"Belge? Our evil father, from whom we have gained independence?

Now, our new father, a son of our land, Mobutu, is planning on wiping out every trace of colonialization; he plans to change all of the names of our cities and towns to African names; he even commands that we change our own names to African names," he said with an animus that frightened Catrin. She was more frightened when he asked the next question.

"Are you alone?" he said, his bloodshot, yellowed eyes peering evilly from the rearview mirror.

She became more and more distraught as he left the Leopoldville Highway, pushing the aging heap through slums that reeked of open sewers and incomprehensible poverty. She cringed when he would stop and speak to a comrade in Lingala, which she didn't understand, and the person would laugh and peer into the car, observing her as one would observe an animal in the zoo.

Finally, he stopped in front of a once-gaily painted building, with a billboard nailed to the roof that stated: "The Ro ale Leopoldville—Exquisite Accommodations." She thought that it would seem much more exquisite if the *y* was not missing from the word *Royale*.

She exited the car without his assistance.

"How much?" she said, digging in her purse.

"That will be fifty francs, mademoiselle," he said, reaching out with his long-fingered hand.

"Okay. And how much is the tip?"

"That will be fifty francs also, mademoiselle." He grinned, still holding out his hand.

"That is ridiculous. You haven't done anything but drive."

"Yes, but you would not allow me to help you with your baggage."

"Then help me with it now. Get my baggage out of the boot of your car!"

"Not unless you pay me my tip," he said, racing his engine as if he were about to drive away.

"Okay, okay. Here are your other fifty francs," she said, slapping the money into his waiting palm.

He shut off the engine, hopped out of the car, opened the trunk, and threw her luggage into the dust.

He spat out a phrase in Lingala as he reentered the car.

"What was that you said?"

"I said that it was a pleasure to serve you," he laughed as he started the automobile and spun out, spraying her with dust and road grime.

Other than the dilapidated sign, one could not discern that the building was actually a hotel.

"Welcome, madame, to the Royal Leopoldville Hotel. My name is Roger, and I will be of service to you," said the thin black man with the very white, gap-toothed smile.

"Thank you, sir. Is my room ready?" said Catrin, dead tired from her long flights and the frightening taxi ride, miserable in the monstrous heat, depressed at the lack of amenities.

"Oh yes, yes. It is ready," he said as she signed the register and paid in cash; all that was accepted. "Unfortunately, I must warn you that we have no hot water, and the lights go off and on periodically. Also, at the moment we have no conditioned air, but we have fans that work well," he said.

"But only when the electricity is on, right?" she said, fanning herself with a travel brochure. She felt as if he was being more than a little disingenuous and feared the worst as far as her accommodations were concerned.

"I will double-check to see if your room is ready. You must be very tired from your journey," he said as he raced towards the stairs. He turned quickly and flashed another bright smile at the stair steps.

"Elevator is broke," he said as he took the steps two at a time, barely stretching his long legs.

Catrin made her way through the shoddy lobby, which was overseen by a couple of scrawny chickens, into the "bar." A boy, about thirteen, was wiping glasses with a grimy rag.

"Would you like something to drink, madame?" he said.

"Yes, I would. Do you have any gin?"

"Maybe. Let me look," he said, as he flung open the doors to a gouged and dusty cupboard.

"Oh yes. We have just a little left," he said, as he removed a dusty bottle of Gordon's Dry London Gin. There was about two inches of what she supposed was gin in the bottle.

"That will do. I think there is enough for a double in there and I will have all of it, in a large glass, with ice and tonic," she said.

He smiled a practiced, gratuitous smile.

"We have no ice and no tonic. But I do have cold water," he said, opening the door to a battered refrigerator and withdrawing a stone pitcher.

"Very well," she sighed and wished she were on the Champs, sipping a cool drink at her favorite tabac.

After a long while, the boy slid two half-full glasses in front of her.

"Sorry, no large glasses," he said.

She reluctantly took a sip from the first glass and winced.

"Something wrong?" said the boy, who was wiping down the bar with the same rag he used to wipe glasses.

She was about to fire off a rude remark when the bellman/desk clerk and whatever else returned.

"I must apologize; your room is not ready, but it will be ready within the next hour," he said, grinning like he'd just told a joke.

Catrin chugged her first drink down and started on the second.

"Well, it looks like I've finished off your gin supply, got any vodka?" she asked the counter boy, who shrugged and began searching the cupboard.

Two hours had passed, and Catrin was getting sloshed, drinking portions of every type of alcohol that comprised the bar. It was getting dark when Roger, the jack-of-all trades, returned.

"Your room is ready, madame," he said with the pride and professional tone of a Conde Nast–trained concierge. Catrin sighed heavily, slid off the wobbly bar seat, and followed him.

The washroom was revolting: a dirty towel draped over a crooked rack; a moldy shower curtain; there was no toilet paper beside the filthy toilet, although there was a partly used roll and a small box of cleaning supplies stored in the non-working bidet.

"This is our communal washroom. Hopefully, you have brought your own toiletries, because they are in short supply here," he said unapologetically. The door was open to her room at the other end of the hallway. Roger ushered her into her room, which was long ago painted a morbid pea-green. There was a fan blowing from the corner, issuing a weak breeze that failed to flutter the flimsy, stained window shades. Gallant as ever, Roger set her luggage down and held out his hand. But when he noticed the shocked look on her face, which was quickly turning to anger, he departed quickly with the comment, "Please don't try to take the elevator to the first floor."

Drunk and exhausted, Catrin started to fall face forward on her bed, but wisely decided to turn the covers down. If she hadn't been so tired, she would have screamed at the sight of hordes of bedbugs scurrying in crevices of the gray, wrinkled sheets, eager to feed on her blood.

"Mon Dieu!" she yelled as she picked up her luggage and struggled out the door.

She spent the night sticking to a faux-leather coach that featured a leaping antelope embossed on the back. As Roger had warned, the electricity had failed, and it was sweltering in the lobby. Despite the abysmal conditions she managed to catch snatches of sleep, but was awakened as an occasional passerby wandered through the open doors. Once she was shaken awake by an old woman who tried to sell her a radio. Near dawn the power came back, bringing to life the fans that circulated the cool morning air nicely. She had just fallen into a deep, exhausted sleep when she was awakened by a hand touching her shoulder gently. Through blurry vision, she noticed that it was a white man's hand.

"You must be miserable. Come with me; the Land Rover has air conditioning and it's clean. You can sleep all the way back to Yamboki, and I will drive slowly," said the driver, who pulled her gently to an upright position.

"Merci" was all that Catrin could utter as the man walked her to the vehicle. A waiting nun opened the back passenger door, and Catrin crawled in, immediately comforted by the cool interior, and thankful that she was being cared for. The man hurried back to the hotel.

"Young man, has the madame's bill been taken care of?" asked the man.

"Yah suh. Did she have an enjoyable stay?" said Roger, displaying a massively white grin.

"Yes. She said it was like Disneyland," said the man as he carted the luggage to the Land Rover.

Roger's grin faded as the Land Rover pulled away.

"Didneyland? What is dis Didneyland?" he said to himself, as he squashed a roach between the pages of the guest register.

Chapter 15

THE ROAD TO YAMBOKI

The road back to Yamboki felt like a ride at Disneyland: serpentine and curvy, bumpy, and full of surprises. "Whoa," yelled the driver for the third time, as a youngster bolted out of the underbrush in front of the vehicle. The nun chuckled as the vehicle swerved violently. "The children are bad enough obstacles, but the goats and chickens are primary hindrances," she laughed, as the driver regained control of the vehicle.

"I ran over a couple of banty roosters last month. I paid a hefty price for them, just to shut the owner up. He made more of a ruckus than the chickens," said the man.

Catrin managed a weak smile, noting that the man was American; his accent reminded her of the downed flier's South Carolina inflection during the war.

"Forgive us for not making introductions, Dr. de Jong; my name is Mother Frederika, of the nursing order Daughters of the Sacred Heart," said the nun, who was quite jovial despite the bone-jarring ride and the probable discomfort of her heavy habit.

"My name is Bowman Rafferty. I am here to show these folks how to grow more sustainable crops," said Bowman over his shoulder. His words were unheard by Catrin, who had fallen sound asleep, her head resting in Mother Frederika's lap, lovingly caressed by the work-worn hands of the motherly nun.

She awoke in a semi-dark room. Slants of sunlight peeked through cracks in the wooden blinds, and the rumble of a generator nearly drowned out the sweet sounds of children playing nearby.

She wondered how long she had been sleeping, and stretched out the kinks in her bones. The sheets were cool, smelling of starch and cleanliness. She felt cleaner too, and was smelling the odor of soap on her forearm when she was startled by a soft voice.

"I gave you a nice sponge bath. But you have a shower when you are ready, Doctor."

The nun, petite in stature, had beautiful brown eyes like Catrin's. And her complexion, beautifully unblemished, another reflection of her soul, was olive in color.

"This is my room?" said Catrin, straining her eyes in the semi-dark as she scanned her surroundings.

"Yes, my child. Would you like for me to open the blinds to give you a better perspective?" said the nun as she floated gracefully to the window.

Sunlight flooded the room, and bright magenta bougainvillea, with a slight wave in the weak breeze, greeted her hospitably outside of the window.

Like a sleepy child, Catrin pointed happily at the plant but said no words.

"You like the bougainvillea? I brought it from Spain," chuckled the nun as she bustled around the immaculate, whitewashed room, which was sparsely furnished: a desk and chair, a rocker, a lamp, an ancient armoire, the bed, and a beautiful crucifix that graced the top of the door. There was also a small bookcase filled with her reference books, and a framed photo of her and Margot.

"I hope you do not mind, but I took the liberty to unpack your things. We washed and pressed your clothing," she said, opening the squeaky door to the armoire, revealing a shelf of neatly folded clothing and some apparel hung on precisely spaced hangers.

"What time is it?" said Catrin, rubbing her eyes.

"It is nearly six o'clock in the evening. We will eat in an hour, after we feed the children. Are you hungry, my child?"

"Yes, I am. I can't believe that I've slept all day," she said, swinging her feet lazily over the side of the bed. The nun laughed heartily.

"You have slept for nearly two days, my dear. If you'd like, I will send someone to escort you to the dining hall in an hour. By the way, my name is Sister Cecelia, and I thank God for your safe arrival, Doctor," she said as she gently closed the door behind her.

The cool concrete floor felt delightful to Catrin's feet as she padded around the room. The overhead fan, powered by the generator, washed the room with a soothing whirr and a nice breeze. She gazed out of the window at the excited children in the midst of a soccer match. They were all beautifully black, and she was touched by their laughter and natural grace. She winced at their rough play, and was impressed that no one whined when they were kicked in the shin; but then again, no one wore shoes so it lessened the effect of the blows. One of the smaller children did receive a direct hit from a larger boy, sending him tumbling head over heels in the dust. The little fellow did not cry, however; he lay on the ground for a while in order to recover his lost breath. She noticed a man who was walking from the fields at the perimeter of the village: a white man. He hastened his steps when he saw the prostrate form of the child. He stooped to the boy and spoke to him as the other children gathered round, some of them draping their arms affectionately over the man's shoulders. He scooped the boy in his arms, hugged him firmly, and spoke in his ear. The child pulled back and proffered a beautiful grin, squeezed the man's neck tightly, and squirmed away to rejoin his comrades in the match. Catrin remembered the man as her driver, but couldn't recall his name.

She was delighted to discover her shower, which was located in a cubbyhole around the corner from the armoire. It was a crude contraption lined with stone, but clean. It took her a while to figure out how to use it; at the pull of a cord, water was fed from a container on the roof to a nozzle. Attached to the nozzle was a small bucket with a perforated bottom. The spray of water, heated well from the noonday sun, felt healing as she scrubbed her skin. She laughed out loud as she dried herself off with a worn but fresh-smelling Turkish towel.

"This is a far cry from the Royal Leopoldville," she said aloud, and distant laughter from the gang of soccer players emphasized her statement.

She felt as fresh and rested as she had been in a long time, hoping that her attire was appropriate for supper: a freshly pressed white blouse with capped sleeves, tan pants, and brown suede boots that would eventually get plenty of use during her service. Her stomach rumbled.

I am famished, I hope we eat soon, she thought, and in answer to her silent plea, there was a tap on the door.

It was her driver, who had exchanged his work clothes for clean work clothes; he was tan and healthy looking and a slight smile broke through his solemn expression.

"Remember me? I'm Bowman Rafferty. And I'm here to escort you to supper, Dr. de Jonge."

"Bowman Rafferty. I saw you today as you comforted that little boy during the soccer match."

"Little Ngunno? That little feller gets beat around quite a bit. But he always dusts himself off and carries on. He reminds me of my son, Durand. Actually all of them do in one way or another. That's why I love them so much," said Bowman as they crossed the small, sun-baked plaza.

As they were nearing the dining hall, the screen door exploded with a fan blast of children, whooping and yelling as they raced for their homes and the soccer pitch. A few of the smaller ones hung around the front of the building as the nun, recognized by Catrin as the nun in the Land Rover, and a small-statured man, presented them with biscuits and other leftovers.

"Here you are, my babies, take these home, and if you get hungry in the night, you can nibble on them," said Mother Frederika lovingly.

A little fellow with a distended belly placed one of the biscuits in his raggedy britches pocket and asked for more.

"Is that little Innocent? He has five older brothers and sisters, and I'm sure they will take a biscuit from him. Give him another and he will have the one in his pocket all for himself," laughed the man, as Mother Frederika deferred to his request. He smiled a wide smile as the children scurried away down the dusty path. And his smile broadened more when he noticed the approach of Catrin and Bowman.

"Ahh! It is Sleeping Beauty, and the good man Bowman," he said, taking her hand and kissing it.

"You have met Mother Frederika. I am your host and your friend, Father Pascal. Welcome to Yamboki, Dr. de Jonge," he said, sweeping his arm gallantly towards the door held open by Mother.

The dining hall was buzzing with a myriad of accents as they entered: Dutch, French, African, German, Spanish, and Catrin was embarrassed as the commotion died down appreciatively at her presence.

"Ladies and gentlemen, please provide a warm welcome for our newest colleague, Dr. Catrin de Jonge from Antwerp!" said Father Pascal, and there was an immediate reply of generous applause, "oohs," and "aahs" as he escorted her to a seat near the head of the table. Bowman sat next to Mother Frederika as Father Pascal raised his hand for silence.

Everyone bowed their heads at the gesture.

"Bless us, oh Lord, and these gifts which we are about to receive from thy bounty, through Christ our Lord, amen."

The chatter returned as bowls of steaming vegetables and meat, which turned out to be goat, were placed on the table. Father Pascal spoke again as he picked up a bowl of steaming yams.

"I would like to bore some of you with another verse in praise of our friend Bowman Rafferty, from whose hands and God's guidance has provided us with this precious bounty: 'Whoever has a bountiful eye will be blessed, for he shares his bread with the poor. Bless you, Bowman!'"

Another round of applause echoed through the room, and Bowman nodded his head sheepishly. Soon mouths were busy chewing rather than gossiping; the whir of wobbly overhead fans and the clank of silverware were predominant sounds in the room.

After the meal, a calabash filled with fermented nsamba (vin de palme) was passed, with everyone including all of the nuns filling their glasses and cups. "It's made from the sap of our wild date palm trees," said Mother Frederika, red-faced as she poured her second glass. "This is pretty potent stuff. The whole village got drunk at Mass one Sunday when they mistakenly used the fermented instead of the non-fermented version," she said.

"That's true. And I had more converts to Christianity that Sunday than ever before," said Father Pascal to heavy laughter.

After-dinner talk ran to gossip, mostly from some of the men, about rebel activity, alleged mutiny in the Congolese Army, Mobutu's dissolution of Parliament, and foreign nationals seeking refuge in Angola.

"Most of the trouble is centered around Stanleyville; I believe we are quite safe here," said a bearded French doctor, with Medecins Sans Frontières, and he was corrected by a researcher from the United Kingdom.

"You mean Kisangani."

"Forgive me, s'il vous plait, Mr. Mobutu," said the Frenchman, glancing pseudo-reverently at the ceiling, and his sarcasm was greeted with laughter.

Catrin would rather have indulged in a full-bodied Cabernet Sauvignon, but the nsamba fulfilled her need for "relaxation." Everyone seemed relaxed with the exception of Bowman, who listened solemnly instead of talking.

As the guests departed, Father Pascal and Mother Frederika joined her in an informal receiving line. Bowman was the last to welcome her.

"You sure look more relaxed this evening than when I first met you," he said, shaking her hand with a gentlemanly grip.

"I am, and I am still tired after two days of sleeping," she said.

"It could be the nsamba," laughed Mother Frederika.

"By the way, if you're not a Christian, would you consider becoming part of the flock?" suggested Father Pascal, cocking his eyebrow comically. The three of them were laughing as Bowman bid them good evening.

"If you all are wanting some more good yams, I'd better say good night," he said, saluting them as he walked out the door.

"He seems so sad," said Catrin.

"He is a very sad man, but hopefully, he is healing," said Father Pascal.

"Healing? Healing from what?"

"He lost his wife and his son in an automobile accident. His brother was driving," said Mother Frederika, stopping short, realizing she had betrayed Dr. Robert Benton's confidence not to mention the incident.

"I was under the impression that his son is still alive," said Catrin.

Father Pascal pounded his chest above his heart.

"He is. In here."

Father Pascal and Mother Frederika were veterans of service on the Dark Continent: enlisting converts to their doctrine, healing hundreds of indigenous people both spiritually and physically, with the aid of volunteers from many professions and organizations.

"How long have we been here, Mother?" said Father Pascal as he poured them both steaming cups of coffee.

"I have been here eleven years. And I believe you were here five years before me," she said, as she blew the steam off the lip of her cup.

"I believe your calculations are correct, Mother Frederika," said Father Pascal as he sat across from her at the dining-hall table. They were quiet for a while, silently remembering their adventurous experiences, and the people who had entered and departed their lives.

"If my memory serves me correctly, we have been here through several rebellions, and there have been many frightening moments. But today, with the country being far from stable, I have learned not to be frightened because my faith in God has bolstered my bravery," he said.

She chuckled.

"I feel the same way. And you are correct, we have been here through both the Simba and the Kwilu rebellions. I was terribly frightened when my Belgian and Italian sisters were taken hostage in Stanleyville, suffering horrible atrocities; I prayed continually for their release, and I prayed for God to let me know if I should stay to serve the poor and downtrodden."

"Your prayers were answered on both counts. Our sisters were released and you're still here," said Father Pascal, stories of several thousand civilians including hundreds of Europeans who were massacred during the rebellions sharp in his mind.

"Actually, we've been pretty lucky, including the blessed people who have volunteered to help us accomplish our mission. No one has been killed on purpose, to my memory, which isn't getting any better," said Mother, as she rose and started turning off the lights in the dining room.

"We lost that German engineer from hemorrhagic fever, and we've had plenty of people nearly succumb to sickness, but I agree, we have been blessed," said Father Pascal as he followed behind her, straightening tables and chairs.

As they walked out of the building, he tested her.

"Are you sure you would not like to lavish in the luxury and the safety of a convent back in Brussels?"

She answered him with a serious request.

"Father, if anything ever happens to me, please ensure that I am buried here to signify my love for this continent to the end."

"I promise," he said, patting her lovingly on the shoulder.

Chapter 16

EXAMINING THE CULTURE

atrin did not have the luxury of melting slowly into the pool of service in Yamboki. There was too much to do, and every minute counted, since deployments for most of the volunteers was minimal—with the exception of some of the spiritual advisors like Father Pascal and Mother Frederika, whose stays were indefinite. In addition to getting to know her colleagues, which were made up of doctors, engineers, agriculture experts, and a small group of scientists, Catrin was kept busy tending to a myriad of wounds and ailments suffered by the villagers, inoculations, and of course, identifying risk factors for diseases, known and unknown, and targets for preventative health care. Her first real challenge came within her second week in Yamboki.

Charles Bakalulindi was not a resident of Yamboki. He was a native of nearby Uganda, where he lived with his parents. They had left him with his mother's sister in Yamboki for a few days while they visited other relatives in the Congo. He played with his cousins for only a day before he became feverish and experienced violent diarrhea and vomiting. When they brought him to the clinic, he had a raised rash on his upper body, and his eyes were red.

"How long has he been like this?" said Catrin as she examined the boy, whose face was devoid of expression.

"Two days," said his aunt, whose brow was furrowed with worry.

Catrin had taken precautions to don a mask, gown, and latex

gloves for the examination, and insisted that everyone in the room follow her example. As she continued the examination, she noticed two puncture wounds in the boy's right forearm.

"Do you know what caused these wounds?"

"He said he was bitten by a green monkey in Uganda," replied his aunt.

Catrin's eyes widened and she immediately gave a command.

"I would like everybody out of the room while I finish this exam," she commanded.

From her work, she knew that green monkeys were suspected of carrying a filovirus called Marburgvirus that fostered highly contagious, deadly Marburg hemorrhagic fever.

Over the next two days, she treated Charles with intravenous fluids, and solutions with electrolytes, tested him for malaria, meningitis, hepatitis, even cholera. She also took blood samples to be tested for viral hemorrhagic fevers, particularly Marburgvirus. With limited lab equipment, she sent that sample to a lab in Belgrade, Yugoslavia, for confirmation. She was extremely worried about the spread of contagion and concerned that it might take a month for the results to come back.

The boy remained mostly mute and expressionless, and his fever was outrageously high.

"Charles, Charles, I wish I knew how to help you," said Catrin, as an undercurrent of concerned conversation from the boy's relatives was heard outside on the clinic porch. Mother Frederika spoke to Catrin in hushed tones.

"Dr. Catrin, several years ago, a German engineer passed away here from hemorrhagic fever, could this be the same strain?"

"I don't know. If this is Marburgvirus, it's more deadly than any of the other filoviruses. About a year ago, thirty-one people died in Germany and Yugoslavia. They said it all started from lab workers handling green monkey tissue in the university town of Marburg."

Later, while Catrin was preparing another test for the boy, Mother

Frederika knocked at her door. It was difficult to determine her expression through the mask on her face. But her voice was tinged with sorrow.

"I am sorry to say that Charles is dead. I've notified Father Pascal, and I will also notify poor Charles' family."

"Thank you, Mother. Please tell the family that Charles must be buried promptly and safely to avoid spreading of contagion. If they are not willing to cooperate, tell them they are breaking the law," said Catrin, who was expecting this to happen.

Dikembe, a respected man in the village, and Bowman hastily dug a grave, and Father Pascal comforted the mourning family, who first insisted that the body be taken back to Uganda for burial, but relented when told of the horrible consequences of not burying the boy immediately. Dikembe also enlisted the help of a woodworker to build a casket for the deceased.

The day the casket was delivered to the clinic, mourners gathered outside, members of the family moaning and sometimes wailing at the loss of their loved one. But knowing the strong possibility of sickness or death from contact with the deceased, no one dared go near the body. Father Pascal, Mother Frederika, and Catrin, and other medical personnel were struggling to wrap the body safely when Bowman appeared at the doorway.

"Dikembe borrowed a donkey and a cart. We will take him to the cemetery," he said, as he approached the body and helped place the boy in the casket.

"Bowman, please be sure to wash your hands and arms thoroughly," said Catrin. He nodded but didn't answer in his concern to transport the casket to the cart.

The road was lined with villagers, some singing, many crying as

Bowman, Dikembe, and Father Pascal guided the donkey cart in the direction of the cemetery. When they arrived, members of the immediate family were ushered to the gravesite, while everyone else stayed back a respectful distance.

The family sang two songs before Father Pascal continued with the service. Knowing that the Ugandan family was Baptist, out of respect, he opted to perform an ecumenical service at the gravesite. His ending prayer was brief, and beautiful:

"To You, oh Lord, we humbly entrust this child, Charles, so precious in Your sight, take him into Your arms and welcome him into paradise where there will be no sorrow, no weeping nor pain, but the fullness of peace and joy with Your Son and the Holy Spirit, forever and ever, Amen."

After the prayer, the coffin was gently lowered with ropes into the grave. The family filed by stoically, throwing fistfuls of red dirt into the hole. As they filtered away from the site, Father Pascal, Dikembe, and Bowman picked up the shovels. Bowman stopped them.

"I'd appreciate it if you'd allow me to do this," he said. They offered no argument, knowing that he was not a man who asked favors of anyone, and that this ritual meant something to him.

It had rained recently, and the dirt was heavy with moisture, each shovelful landing with a heavy *thunk* on Charles Bakalulindi's crude coffin. Bowman was drenched with sweat and his shovel handle and spade were weighted heavily with clay, but he kept a steady pace, humming an old hymn in his head, a requiem of sorts, for the deceased, and a rhythm to follow as the hole was filled. Several times, Dikembe started to help him, but Father Pascal held him back. "This is a tribute," said Father Pascal, and Dikembe stepped back reluctantly.

Catrin watched from a distance as Bowman filled in the grave by himself and was intrigued by the action.

The clinic was scrubbed from top to bottom with soap, water, and bleach. The villagers were preached to about the absolute need for cleanliness, and the necessity of frequent hand washing. And when the pall of a dead child hanging over the village began to retreat, a semblance of normality returned as they waited for the results of the tests that were sent to Europe. Finally they received word from Prague, stating that Charles had suffered from hemorrhagic fever, but the virus was not the Marburg strain.

"They say that it is Crimean Congo hemorrhagic fever, and it is tick-borne, not from bats or monkeys," said Catrin as she read the report to several of her colleagues.

At supper one evening, Father Pascal praised the bravery and Godliness of everyone who took action to protect the villagers and their colleagues during the crisis, and they good-naturedly gave themselves a round of applause.

"I guess that sidestepping monkeys, fruit bats, and ticks is an important part of our protocol," said one of the Brits, his dark humor appreciated by his colleagues.

Later, Catrin asked Bowman a question that had been troubling her since the incident.

"Bowman, I was wondering, why did you insist on filling the grave by yourself?"

He sipped his coffee, and paused before answering.

"I guess you could call it my way of saying good-bye to a fallen child," he said.

She suspected that he was speaking of a child in addition to Charles Bakalulindi. And she began to fall in love with the sad and noble man.

Chapter 17

OWANDI

Catrin had slept well to the thrumming of rain on her roof, and awakened early to get ready for her visit to the leper colony. She was showered, dressed, and ready to go, but it was still too early to meet Father Pascal at the clinic. She sat on her bed, reopened the envelope, and reread the letter she had recently received from Margot.

> Dear Mamma,
> Pappa dropped me off at Jolein's and spent a few days working around the farm. He got sunburned and also pulled a muscle in his leg as he was diving into the pond. He didn't complain, but sure looked pitiful as he limped around. He did complain a little though about getting older. He was very sad and worried about you being gone and spoke about how much he loves you and me. He took me to the cemetery to see the graves of my grandmother, grandfather, and of his younger brother Armandus. He was very sad, and we spent about an hour cleaning up around them. Please be careful in the Congo and bring me back an African mask.
> Love you,
> Margot

"I wish I could believe all of that," she said to herself as she searched for her knapsack.

The rain, a straight-down deluge, was relentless. She was packing medications and sample kits into her knapsack when Bowman came stomping onto the porch of the clinic.

"Not a good day for working in the fields, but we needed the rain. Now, I wish it would stop," he said, slipping out of his soaked poncho and hanging it on a hook outside the door.

"So, what are you going to do, sleep the day away?" she said jokingly.

"Actually, I thought I'd ask if you needed any help."

"I can always use some help. Father Pascal and I are going to visit Owandi today. Would you like to join us?"

Bowman didn't hesitate to reply.

"I welcome the opportunity. I've been here quite a while and haven't had a chance to visit. Do they need food?"

"They always need food."

"Wait for me. I've gathered a lot of vegetables, and some fruit to examine. They are all in good shape."

"We'll wait on you."

The downpour continued, forming muddy rivers into the rutted, dusty roads, making the normally short trip to Owandi difficult and lengthy.

"What are my chances of contracting leprosy?" said Bowman, as Father Pascal maneuvered the Land Rover expertly through the ruts and the mud.

"Most of our patients suffer from the tuberculoid form of the disease and it's less contagious. You are fairly safe, unless you come into close and repeated contact with nose and mouth drops from someone with untreated leprosy," said Father Pascal.

"You'll be fine. All of our patients are being treated with Clofazomine and Rifampicin, and they are not contagious," assured Catrin.

Having little understanding of medicine or terminology, but possessing respect for her expertise, Bowman took Catrin's words for the gospel.

The place appeared abandoned as the Land Rover groaned and spun through the quagmire that was the main artery that coursed through the village. Occasionally a shadowy form would appear briefly in a doorway, then dematerialize into the darkness of a decrepit shack. Father Pascal parked the vehicle on a flat rock: an island in the midst of a rain-saturated bog.

"I believe this is one of our first stops," he said as he led them to a rundown shanty and knocked on the screen door, which hung crookedly on its hinges. A pig met him at the door, then a woman, whose face was covered by a stained scarf.

"We have come with medicine for you and your children, and we have some food too," said Father Pascal, and the woman welcomed him with a wave of her bandaged hand as the pig squealed and bolted out the door into the rain.

They followed primarily the same drill as they made their way from home to home: Father Pascal speaking the local patois efficiently, administering to spiritual needs; Catrin dispensing medicine and inoculations; while Bowman held the children and calmed them. Catrin was taken by how the children reacted to his goodness, and his sincere desire to hold them despite some of their horrible afflictions.

Darkness was on the horizon, and they were getting weary as they stopped at the last house on the perimeter of the village. They were met at the entrance by a boy with bandaged hands and feet, and multiple skin sores. He had his thin arm around a younger boy who was obviously blind. The boy clung to him in fear.

Bowman noticed the ghostly forms of many people in the darkened interior, sitting still as statues in the fading gray light. For a moment he was spooked; this was a scene out of a horror movie. Catrin tended to the older boy, who refused to loosen his grip on his blind brother. Then, she turned her attention to the blind child, who started to cry. He cried harder when Bowman sat him in his lap. The older brother still refused to release his hold on the child, and Bowman picked him up with one hand and sat him on his other knee. The smaller child continued to whimper, but stopped when Bowman sang to him in a soft voice. As he sang, Bowman remembered an instance from his childhood.

Bernard was wailing like a banshee, and his mother was distraught at the sight of the nasty lump on his forehead. Bowman was trying to comfort him, without much success.

"How did this happen, Bowman?" she said as she examined the lump closely.

"I fell down," screamed Bernard, clinging frantically to his brother.

Bowman was incredulous at the lie. He had thrown a rock, not meaning to hit Bernard, but clobbered him in the forehead. Bernard was protecting him.

"Well, let me make up an ice pack. Bowman, you look after your brother till I get back."

"What do you want me to do?"

"Anything that will make him stop that screaming. His daddy will bust his behind if he won't," she said nervously as she bustled out of the room.

He held his brother close.

"Please, Bernard, stop crying or Daddy will spank you," he said, but Bernard continued yowling.

Desperate, Bowman sang a song that he knew was Bernard's favorite from Sunday school.

"Jesus loves the little children, all the little children of the world..."

Bernard stopped crying and amidst sniffles, sang the chorus along with Bowman.

"Red and yellow, black and white, we are precious in his sight, Jesus loves the little children of the world."

When they finished the song, Jud appeared in the doorway, scowling.

"What's the matter? Can't you put one foot in front of the other without falling?" he admonished, then he shook his head disgustedly as he turned and stormed away.

Bernard looked into Bowman's soul with watery eyes.

"Am I precious, Bowman?"

"Sure, we all are."

"I don't feel precious," said Bernard, as their mother appeared with an ice pack.

"Red and yellow, black and white, we are precious in his sight, Jesus loves the little children of the world," sang Bowman, his voice cracking at the end. The blind child was calm now that Catrin was finished with the examination, his brother still clinging to him.

"That should do it," said Catrin, packing up her medical kit, swabbing herself with alcohol.

"Here, Bowman, you might want to use some of this also," she said, passing the bottle to him.

He sat the boys on the floor, and the older boy kissed his brother on the cheek.

"You take good care of your brother, hear?" said Bowman, and Catrin thought she heard his voice tremble at the end of the sentence.

"I'll clean myself up at the car," he said, and she could barely make out his face in the darkness as he exited the shack.

They travelled mostly in silence back to Yamboki.

"So Bowman, what was your impression of the trip today?" said Father Pascal.

Bowman paused a lengthy time before answering.

"It was smelly; it was heartbreaking; but it was good," he said, and Catrin admired him.

"You are good, Bowman," said Father Pascal, as the lights of Yamboki beckoned to them.

The rains ended, leaving a torrent of mud that clung tenaciously to everything, covering the children's feet and legs and drying to resemble boots of tan, drenching clothing with splatters and causing comical accidents that were the source of great stories and much laughter at the dinner table.

Father Pascal was crying with hilarity as he told the tale.

"She tripped coming out of the clinic and fell face first in the mud at the foot of the steps. I ran to the edge of the steps, just as a pig ran to her and stared at her out of curiosity. She rolled over, looked at the pig, and then at me. "Get your ass over here and help me out, before this swine thinks I'm his cousin!" she said, spitting mud from her mouth.

The audience howled along with Father Pascal, as Catrin turned beet red.

"I am sorry for that outburst, Father. I was just…just…"

"Pissed?" interrupted Bowman, and the group roared again, for it was unlike Bowman to join in the revelry and quip with the rest of them. Catrin, who was sitting next to him, unconsciously hugged his arm, showing her appreciation for his participation and her overall admiration for him. Bowman smiled, helped himself to another glass of vin de palme, and leaned in to her. He raised his glass.

"Here's to the prettiest cousin ever to visit Yamboki," he said.

"Cheers!" yelled members of the unique group as they clicked their odd assortment of glasses and mugs together, in the midst of ring-ing laughter. Father Pascal started the chorus of "She's a Jolly Good Fellow" and everyone joined in but Bowman. His head was humming with "Jesus Loves the Little Children"—the replay of the sorrowful story of a precious sibling.

Both of them were a little tipsy from the vin de palme as they hop-scotched erratically, laughing like children, jumping from board to rock to other solid objects placed along the road to help avoid being inundated in the swamp of mud. Finally, they came to her quarters.

"Well, good night, Catrin. I enjoyed your company this evening."

"You too, Bowman. And thank you for that toast you raised to me, although I doubt its sincerity."

"Oh, it was sincere, I'm just not very good at it."

He was silent for a moment. Made a faltering step toward her, then, stepped back.

"Did you want to say something?" said Catrin, hoping that he would ask her if he could come in, wishing that he would make love to her.

They were quiet until Catrin finally found her voice.

"I believe that you are good at a lot of things, Bowman. You just have to let yourself go," she said, placing her hand on his chest, hoping that he was aware of the innuendo.

"I understand what you're saying, Catrin. I wish I could let go, but there is too much holding me back. Good night, I have to be up early tomorrow and I think that vin de palme is going to make it difficult."

She was angry as she watched him disappear in the moonlight. "C'est la vie," she whispered, berating herself for being selfish and feeling somewhat like a tramp.

He looked like hell when he walked into the dining hall early the next morning. But so did everyone else who'd attended the impromptu party the evening before. Coffee was flowing copiously instead of vin de palme, and Father Pascal, bags under his eyes, hair askew, offered him a cup.

"What do you call this in Tennessee, Bowman?" he said, handing him the steaming cupful.

"Coffee," said Bowman, eliciting titters instead of guffaws from the hung-over crew.

A weak cheer went up as Catrin came in. Unlike the others, she appeared fresh as a flower. She flushed a bit when she saw Bowman, embarrassed by her come-on to him at her doorstep the night before. The only seat left at the table was next to him, and after getting her coffee, she sat by him reluctantly. As chatter continued amongst the men and women regarding their workdays, Bowman spoke to her softly.

"I'm sorry, Catrin. I can't bring myself to…to…you know. I'm not worthy of you," he said, as Dikembe pecked on the door and waved for him to come out.

She wanted to say he was wrong, that it was the other way around, but was afraid that the others would hear her, or discern how she felt about him through her actions.

As he got up from the table, he smiled at her.

"I may feel better about things one day," he said as he walked out the door.

She smiled as she sipped her coffee, knowing that Bowman was lying through his teeth.

You know that you are worthy, Bowman. You're just hopelessly in love with someone else, she thought with no malice.

Chapter 18

TRIP TO KINSHASA

"**H**ave we got everything?" said Father Pascal.

"We don't have much; have to save room for the load coming back," said Bowman, as he situated himself in the driver's seat.

"After my last visit there, I didn't ever want to see it again," laughed Catrin, as she climbed in to the backseat of the Land Rover. Father Pascal shut her door, then settled himself in the front passenger seat.

"*Bon voyage*," yelled the nuns and the villagers as the trusty Land Rover dug into the rutted road leading out of Yamboki.

The trio was on their way to Kinshasa (formerly, Leopoldville) that seemed to line the banks of the Congo River indeterminately. Their mission was to report to the Kinshasa Port Railway Station to pick up medical supplies that had been sent from the U.S., Belgium, and France. It was considered a dangerous mission because of the constant state of unrest inherent to the sprawling city-province once known as Kin La Belle, "Kinshasa the Beautiful," and now called "Kin la Poubelle," "Kinshasa the Trash Bin," for obvious reasons. Slums made up the major portions of the large city, which was endemic with sickness, gangs, muggings, robberies, slavery, genocide, rapes, kidnappings, and even incidences of cannibalism. Adding to the chaos was the disintegration of the peacekeepers—soldiers who were currently rioting for back pay.

Bowman didn't speak of his Browning-designed .45-caliber service pistol secreted in his day pack, for fear of disturbing Catrin and gentle Father Pascal. Likewise, Catrin had concealed her trusty Luger in her bag.

They bumped along the back roads for a long while until they came upon the Kinshasa Highway, which runs through the Congo into Uganda and beyond.

"Would you like for me to drive, Bowman? I am more familiar with this road than you are," said Father Pascal, who served several years as a missionary in this region. Bowman took him up on his offer, and at the first wide spot in the road, changed places with him. Although he was familiar with the road, Father Pascal was flabbergasted to see where the roadway was already being taken over by the jungle in some places. Soon, they were mired in heavy traffic, mostly trucks of every kind, barreling wickedly toward the looming skyline. Bowman was glad he was a passenger instead of the driver. He'd been to this city before, on his arrival and to pick up Catrin, and both instances were nerve-wracking experiences.

Mountains of garbage and hastily erected slums disguised the former routes to which Father Pascal was accustomed.

"Please forgive me. Things have changed so much in such a short period of time," he said, as he perused an old map of the ever-changing city.

"Maybe we should ask one of these children," said Catrin as she rolled her window down. They were suddenly overwhelmed by the stench of open sewers and the onslaught of screaming street children with their hands outstretched.

Claude was too interested in his find to join the army of children besieging the Land Rover. Besides, they wouldn't have welcomed him into their ranks. Because of his horrible disfigurement, he was an outcast, accused of being a witch, probably, because of his uncanny ability to exist on his own in the mean streets from the age of four; it was "magic" that he could survive against these dreadful odds. He picked the rot out of the potato, scraped out what was left of the innards, barely chewed and swallowed them. He was wadding the skin and stuffing his mouth when his dinner was interrupted.

"Hey, you ugly little bastard! Come down off your mountain. We want to eat you!" echoed Fabrice's voice through the canyons of garbage. The request was followed by raucous laughter. Nimble as a monkey, Claude swallowed the potato skin as he clambered higher up the precariously leaning stack of trash. He knew the voice of Fabrice; he knew that there would be horrific consequences if he was caught; the thought of being eaten sent him scampering to the pinnacle of the mountain, where he burrowed like a rat into the depths of the waste.

Fabrice's gang did not have the wherewithal to purchase pistols, but they were feared because they carried a wicked assortment of weapons: knives, ice picks, machetes, vials of acid. And they were quick to use them, with no compassion for their victims—victims like Claude, who was already one of the most careworn victims of the slums of Kinshasa.

"The little rat with teeth growing out of his face has dug himself a nest in the trash. Want to go dig him out?" said Fabrice, a powerfully built teen with tribal scarification etched into his face and shoulders.

"I wouldn't do that. He is a witch, and I might end up being a rat with teeth growing out of my face too," said Ariza, Fabrice's lieutenant. Fabrice started to respond when he heard the commotion across the road.

Although he spoke Lingala, the language of the street, quite fluently, Father Pascal's request was drowned out by the dissonance of desperately hungry children as they begged for alms.

"We are trying to get to Kinshasa Port Railway Station," he said to deaf ears. Suddenly the crowd of children dispersed, flying away like a flock of startled crows.

"Are you lost?" said Fabrice in what he considered a honeyed voice, as the rest of his motley entourage surrounded the vehicle, some brandishing knives at their sides.

"Yes, we are. Will you tell us how to get to the Kinshasa Port

Railway Station?" said Father Pascal, as Catrin fumbled in her bag for the Luger and Bowman retrieved his .45 from his pack.

"We will if you give us money," grinned Fabrice maliciously.

"We have very little money. Will five dollars do?" said Father, and the gang laughed incredulously.

As they were laughing, Ariza broke out Catrin's window with a ball-peen hammer, unlocked the door, and dragged her out of the car.

"I will make you a deal. We will take this white dog bitch, and you will drive away; but first, give me twenty-five dollars," said Fabrice, and as Catrin struggled in the steely grip of Ariza, other gang members gravitated toward them.

The deafening thunder of the .45 filled the air as Bowman emerged from the Rover. The gang scattered like rats at the sound, but Fabrice and Ariza stayed their ground.

"That is a fine gun, white man. I will make you a deal. You give me the gun, and I will spare the life of your woman."

"I don't trust you. Let her go and I'll drop the gun," said Bowman, the big gun steady in his grasp.

"Ariza, slit her throat," commanded Fabrice.

"Wait, wait," pleaded Father Pascal, who was out of the car now, fumbling in his wallet.

"I have 150 dollars. It's all we have. Take it!" he begged, handing over the whole wallet.

Fabrice seemed undisturbed that the gun was still trained on him, as he accepted the wallet eagerly.

"You lied to me. But I will forgive you. That's a nice deal, but not nice enough. I want the gun too."

"Will you let the woman go?" said Bowman.

"Sure. She is yours," said Fabrice, as members of the gang groaned.

"Ariza, bring her around to this side of the car," he ordered, and Ariza complied, dragging Catrin, who was struggling not to whimper, around to the opposite side of the Rover.

"Now give me the gun," said Fabrice, and Bowman complied reluctantly. Ariza still refused to release Catrin from his clutches.

"Let her go!" yelled Bowman, who moved toward Ariza. One of the gang members rushed him and planted an ice pick in his shoulder. Bowman fell to one knee, then staggered to a standing position.

"Let them go, you bastard," he said, stumbling toward Ariza, the ice pick hanging grotesquely from his shoulder.

"We will do with them as we please. But first, I want them to see you die," said Fabrice, taking careful aim at Bowman's head with the .45. Catrin started to cry.

"Please, spare him," she said, barely able to speak as Ariza's forearm pressed against her larynx.

"Give her to me, I want to be the first to comfort her," said Fabrice, and Ariza obeyed, releasing his grip and shoving her in his direction.

"Come to me, white bitch dog. Watch while I destroy your man," he said. Bowman groaned loudly as he yanked the ice pick from his shoulder and charged Fabrice.

"Stop, I'll kill you," screamed Fabrice.

Bowman kept coming.

"What's the difference, you're going to kill me anyway. But I'm going to get a couple of licks in first," said Bowman as he rushed him.

There were gunshots fired from nearby, and the gang scattered.

"Stay where you are and drop the gun," commanded an authoritative voice from the darkness, which was lorded over by the trash heaps.

Fabrice, unsmiling for the first time since the encounter, dropped the .45 as several soldiers materialized. Their leader picked up the pistol and examined it.

"Nice weapon," he mumbled.

"This man and his gang tried to rob us," said Catrin as she examined Bowman's shoulder.

"Yes, we have encountered him many times. He is an animal," said the leader.

"Yes, we know one another. We are friends, correct, Sergeant?" said Fabrice, the smile returning to his face.

"Not anymore," said the sergeant, who calmly shot Fabrice in the head with Bowman's weapon.

"You mind if I keep this?" said the leader calmly, shooting a devious glance at Bowman.

"It's yours," grunted Bowman, as Catrin examined his wound.

"Merci," said the soldier, who nodded to his companions, and they disappeared into the labyrinth of trash mounds.

"Let's get out of here before the gang returns," said Catrin, and she didn't have to ask twice. As Father Pascal drove, she tended to Bowman in the backseat. She gave him a strong pain pill from her medicine kit, and it took effect quickly.

"Those soldiers must have received their back pay," he said. But no one laughed.

Claude enjoyed the spectacle from his perch atop the malodorous heap. He smiled a grotesque smile as he beheld the body of Fabrice, a stream of blood flowing in rivulets from his shattered head. Claude was happy too that he'd found a bag half full of plantain chips. Life was good.

Catrin doctored Bowman as best she could and was able to tend to his wound more professionally once they picked up the medicines and other supplies at the Kinshasa Port Railway Station. She opened stronger samples of pain medication, gave him a tetanus shot, penicillin, and other injections of heavy-duty antibiotics on their way back to Yamboki. While he slept under the influence of the powerful painkillers, she dressed and re-dressed the wound often, checking for infection.

"How is our patient doing?" said Father Pascal, deep concern registering in his eyes, which were reflected in the rearview mirror.

"He's snoring. That means he's alive," said Catrin, as she swabbed pearls of sweat off Bowman's forehead. She continued.

"I've given him better care than what he would have received in a Kinshasa hospital. Besides, he's tough; he'll be alright."

"I'm glad you were along. It would have been perilous to stay in that evil place any longer than we had to," said Father Pascal, squinting as brilliant lights from the oncoming tankers temporarily blinded him.

"I'm glad you were there, and Bowman too," she said, reaching forward and squeezing Father Pascal's shoulder lovingly.

"He is a very brave man, don't you agree?" said Father.

She exhaled deeply.

"I guess so. If 'brave' means you don't care if you live or die."

Bowman moaned as they bumped off the main highway to a side road, and Father Pascal aimed the Land Rover in the general direction of Yamboki. Catrin placed a towel between Bowman's injured shoulder and the back of the seat, and wondered if the drugs prevented him from monitoring their conversation. She turned her attention to Father Pascal for a moment.

"How are you feeling, Father?"

"You wouldn't happen to have a little vin de palme with you, would you?"

They both had a chuckle despite the horror they'd experienced.

Chapter 19

OF THE STARS AND THE RIVER

The Yamboki contingent was flabbergasted at the Kinshasa story, and thankful that their friends had come back to them unscathed, with the exception of Bowman, who, with the devout attention of all of the medical and spiritual personnel, was healing nicely from the ice-pick attack.

Almost as soon as Bowman entered the dining hall, the sisterhood swarmed around him like flies, seating him and asking of his needs. Mother Frederika set a tray in front of him containing his dinner, served prettily in steaming bowls and plates. His comrades laughed and taunted him.

"The old boy is milking this for all he's worth, fellows," said one of the UK docs, and the others agreed loudly.

Mother Frederika placed her hand lightly on Bowman's injured shoulder, and spoke in mock anger.

"I would do the same for any of you. You should learn the importance of service to others," she said, shaking her index finger at them as the door opened. Catrin appeared and headed straight for Bowman.

"How's that shoulder? Let me take a look at it after dinner, okay?"

He turned crimson as the group snickered and snorted at her remarks.

Bowman enjoyed working with Dikembe, a wizened-appearing

older man, bone thin, but possessing the strength and endurance that Bowman failed to realize, even as a strapping youngster.

"Ha! How is that shoulder healing?" shouted Dikembe, as he strolled toward Bowman in their planted field.

"Please, don't say that too loud," said Bowman, placing his finger to his lips.

Dikembe was confused over the comment, but agreed to keep quiet about Bowman's injury. He quickly changed the subject.

"I would like to tell you about my discovery today, Bowman."

"What have you discovered, Dikembe?" said Bowman, sharing the little man's excitement.

"I have discovered that your plan of planting the maize along with molasses grass has made the evil stem borers go away," said Dikembe, smiling, revealing his two front teeth, which were extremely bucked, giving him the appearance of an emaciated cartoon rabbit.

"I told you so," said Bowman, encircling the little man's shoulders with his arm.

"But our success is really due to the work you and your team have put into the project."

In the distance a crew of men were singing as they hoed nitrogen, leaves, wood from tree fallows, pods, and green branches into the soil in preparation for a second planting of the corn.

"My brothers are happy too. Listen to them sing their happiness for having good crops; and for your recovery, Bowman. Oops, I am not supposed to mention that, am I?"

Bowman stopped to listen to the exquisite cadence and harmony, honed through time immemorial, unsullied by influences from other cultures.

"Lutuku y Bene Kanyoka," sang the men, the *thunk* of the hoes in the soft earth providing a heavy back beat to the melody.

"What does that mean?" asked Bowman.

"It means many things to many people. But basically, it means coming out of grief," said Dikembe, smiling his rabbit smile.

Bowman was thankful that Dikembe's words almost always gave him pause to think.

"Let's knock off for today. Tell them they can go home."

Dikembe laughed again.

"Maybe that is why they are singing. You should sing also," he laughed, as he shouted toward the group.

One corner of the sky was cobalt blue and stippled with stars, eagerly encroaching in gradients on the daylight which was still hanging on by an orange thread. Bowman and Dikembe rested from their labors, seated on a hillside overlooking the bottom land that nourished their flourishing maize crop.

"The stars are looking down with favor, Bowman. We have done well," said Dikembe, the last rays of the sun burnishing his broad, black face.

"The stars are interested because the composition of that maize is made up of them," said Bowman, as night gradually overtook the surrendering remnants of daylight. He was intrigued by Dikembe's reply.

"Ha, Bowman. It is taught in my culture that you and I are created from stardust too."

"I believe that. But many creationists would disagree with you."

"What is this creationist?"

"It is a person that believes that only God made the universe and us."

"As it says in the Bible?"

"Yes."

"Is it an offense to God if I don't believe everything that men have written in the Bible?"

"I used to believe so. I don't think I do now."

"I believe that the Bible was meant well, as direction for us to achieve heaven. And I believe that God's hand stirred the pot for the creation of the universe. And that no man could imagine how that great task was done."

"I think you may be right, although I was not taught that way," said Bowman, as cool crept up from the earth, and the tree frogs began to chirp their approval. Dikembe was thoughtful.

"Bowman, do you agree that we are made from the stars?"

"Greater men than you and I have pondered that thought, Dikembe."

Dikembe answered himself, ignoring Bowman's reply.

"Then, if we are made from the stars, we are part of God, no? We are a piece of God? We are a piece of each other?"

Bowman attempted to answer, but was interrupted by Dikembe's musical laugh.

"Then, that makes us brothers, doesn't it?" he said.

Dikembe reached over and rubbed the skin on Bowman's forearm.

"Well, at least cousins," he whooped, and fell back on the grass laughing

He stopped abruptly, his face darkening with the dying light.

"I have a brother, and he is a bad man."

Bowman knew that it was best not to answer, to allow him to go on.

"He joined the rebels, and he is one of their leaders now. He has no God and he kills people in the name of his former leader, Mulele— the rooster who claimed to watch over us chickens."

There was a loud, guttural grunt and squeal that echoed throughout the jungle, startling a flock of screeching storks way beyond the treetops near the lake. They rose in a collective wail of disharmony, their silhouettes fluttering crazily in the dying light, then floating back lazily toward the earth like dry, falling leaves. They settled back into their roosting perches, muttering complainingly amongst themselves.

"What is his name?"

"Mboku."

"Do you hate him for what he is and what he has done?"

"I cannot hate him," said Dikembe incredulously.

"Why?"

"Simply because he was made to be my brother. I cannot control what he has become; that is between him and the universe," said Dikembe as he rose with the agility of a young man.

"I will be seeing you early in the morning, is that okay?"

"Yes. I will see you here," said Bowman, as nocturnal creatures could be heard stirring in the bush.

"Good night, my brother, sleep in the bosom of your ancestors."

"Same to you, my brother," said Bowman, as the word "brother" reverberated in his mind. Deep in thought, he took a separate path in the direction of the river.

Catrin noticed his silhouette on the rise against the darkening sky—tall, lumbering; unmistakably Bowman. She last saw him descending on the path down to the river. She had been uneasy with rumors of the Simba in the neighborhood, and she was still unused to the hoots, growls, and rustling of the night beasts on the move in the surrounding tangle of forest. Now, she was relieved to know that he was coming this way. She folded her clothing neatly, stacking it on the cluster of exposed roots of an Okoumé tree on the riverbank, placing her Luger on top of the clothing. The moon had risen, and filtered through the outstretched arms of the trees hovering above the river. The air was still as death, and even in her nakedness, she failed to gain respite in the muggy ambience. Her body responded delightfully as she slipped into the cool depths of the silvery black pool. Sinking beneath the surface, she relished the liquid world that spoke in muted tones of protectiveness. When she surfaced, a rush of night sounds assailed her ears: life that flourished in the trees, in the water and the jungle floor. And there was his voice—alarmed, mingling unnaturally with the chorus of nature.

"Catrin! You scared the dickens out of me! I thought you were a croc," he said from his half-turned stance in the opposite direction of the river.

"You would dare to face le croise to experience this coolness on your body," she laughed and splashed water playfully toward the bank. "Come in, Monsieur Bowman, and experience the delight," she said.

"Can you see me?" he said nervously.

"I can make out your form, but only slightly," she giggled.

"Alrighty then, I'm comin' in," he said as he stripped down in the moonlight. She could see him plainly. And she admired the vision.

In his eagerness, or perhaps anxiety, Bowman entered the water splashily, with much less grace than Catrin. Her laugh echoed off the narrow banks and trees as he spit and sputtered. He surfaced and stood, up to his waist, in the pool.

"Come over this way; the water is much deeper, perhaps up to your shoulders," she said, beckoning him with a wave of her hand. He declined, shaking his head, spray flying from his hair.

"You were right. This is refreshing," he said.

She held an object up for his inspection in the moonlight.

"I have soap, and I will share it with you, if you don't mind."

"It's not that sissy-smelling French soap, is it?"

She laughed, and he stepped back a step as she approached him.

"No parfum at all. This is Moringa soap, made by Dikembe's wife, Narolie. It has a wonderful natural aroma, if you can detect an aroma at all," she said, tossing him the bar.

He failed to catch the soap, which disappeared momentarily below the surface and popped up like a rubber duck on the face of the silvery pool. He plucked it from the water and smelled it.

"It smells like leaves; very nice," he said as he scrubbed his chest, neck, and arms with the bar.

She laughed again softly, gratified that he was enjoying her gift.

"It's made from leaves that are ground into paste. In good light, it is a beautiful color of green," she said as she moved closer to him. She stopped briefly, sensing his unease—and, in a good-natured way, enjoying it. She ducked under and surfaced behind him.

"Don't turn around, Bowman, I'll wash your back," she said, reaching around him to retrieve the soap from his hand.

"I have to tell you that I'm not used to this. The last and only time I ever went skinny dipping was with Rosalee...that was the summer before Durand was born," he said, as she scrubbed his broad shoulders gently. She noticed that the ice-pick wound had healed over nicely and there was a keloidal scar forming at the site of the healed injury. She traced it gently with her fingers, remaining silent during the examination, then continuing her conversation.

"Oh, I've gone naked swimming and otherwise with many people in my lifetime. Going topless at the North Sea in the summer; changing clothes with my brothers and sisters, even my parents; and of course, with my husband. I believe that we Europeans are more casual than you Americans about nudity—we do not always associate nudity with sex," she said. Bowman wished he could feel more casual about this occasion. But as she scrubbed, he could feel her taut nipples trace his back, and he was becoming extremely bothered.

"Now, duck under, Bowman, and rinse off," she said, touching his shoulder lightly and pushing him down.

In his brief underwater intermission, he was reminded that he hadn't really been touched by a woman since Rosalee's death. He was extremely aroused, and somewhat ashamed of his thoughts as he resurfaced.

She was stepping lithely onto the riverbank, and she was exotic in the moonlight: an alabaster statue come to life.

"Come on out, Bowman. I'll share my towel with you if you'd like," she said, ruffling her hair with the towel.

He waited for a while, hoping to quell his excitement, embarrassed that he would divulge his condition.

She screamed, and he forgot about his timidity as he rushed through the water to the shore.

"Get it! Get it! Get it!" she whimpered, pointing to her buttocks. He knelt quickly, fearing to find a snake attached to her bottom. Not realizing that horrific vision, he exhaled deeply.

"It's a leech. I'll get it," he said, plucking the parasite off her derriere with composure.

"Check me…check me, from head to toe! Please, Bowman, those things are vile, and they disgust me," she whined.

Bowman obliged her request although it was a very difficult task to perform, his excitement exacerbated by her need for him and the intimate body search. When he was finished, she thanked him profusely.

"Bowman. You are my hero," she laughed, only slightly embarrassed, hugging him but stepping away quickly at the sight and feel of his excitement.

"I'm sorry. I couldn't help it. You are a beautiful woman and the first who has ever touched me since…since…"

She was deeply moved by his confession, and his sadness, but refrained from touching him again, at least while they were in their Adam-and-Eve state.

"That's okay, Bowman, perhaps if you were European, you wouldn't feel this way," she laughed and threw him her towel. She admitted to herself that she wouldn't have been displeased if he had taken her. But she admired his innocence and devotion to the memory of his wife.

They both laughed about the incident as they donned their clothes.

"I will not forget this moment for the rest of my life. Do you mind if I hug you now, Bowman?"

"Not at all, Catrin. Thank you for understanding," he said as he enfolded her in his arms. He felt himself becoming aroused again as she brushed his cheek with soft-as-rose-petal lips. She felt his reaction to the stimuli and freed herself from his embrace.

"We had better get back now. I'm surprised that no one from the village responded to my screams," she said as they walked slowly down the path.

"Hell, they're probably scared to come out of their houses," he laughed, and she joined him, delighted to hear him laugh.

Eyes peered at them from the bush as they walked away.

As they came into the clearing, several men were seated around a fire, drinking beer. And much to the couple's relief, they were ignored.

"Probably drunk," he chuckled.

"Thank goodness," she whispered.

"I actually had a good time tonight. Thanks f or the experience," he said, touching her cheek lightly.

"De rien." She smiled, thinking, *Donc mon adversaire me dit*—the French equivalent to "close but no cigar."

"Good night, Rosalee," he said softly as he turned toward his billet.

She smiled once more, noticing that he hadn't realized his indiscretion.

But rather than being offended, she was honored.

Chapter 20

THE HOUSE OF DIKEMBE

Catrin sat down at the table amid the buzz and hum of conversation. Suppertime was the highlight of every busy day and the staff enjoyed the camaraderie immensely: talking about discoveries they had made, families back home, and of course their "family" here, whom they had come to respect and even love through their work. Catrin absentmindedly counted the bodies, and everyone was there, with the exception of Bowman. Father Pascal was keeping count too.

"Does anyone know the whereabouts of Bowman this evening?" he asked.

One of the men on the agriculture team responded.

"He was having dinner with Dikembe and his family this evening, I believe."

There was an undercurrent of "hmmms" in the audience. It was rare that the indigenous people, who were very shy, proffered an invitation to their homes to a white person.

"Well, I hope that big fellow doesn't eat them out of hut and home," said one of the Brits, to everyone's amusement including Catrin's. She was thankful that Bowman had not opted out of communal dinner in an effort to avoid her because of their au naturel meeting the night before.

The sun was still high and scorching as Bowman walked to Dikembe's house, and not many villagers were out at this time of day, just a few children who didn't care about the heat as long as they could spin a hoop along the packed dirt with a stick, or kick a soccer ball made of rags in the road in front of their homes. He noticed men sitting in the shade of their houses playing dominoes, swatting at flies, and laughing as the smoke of their pipes and cigarettes curled above their heads Women were absent from the exterior of their homes, probably making dinner for their families. He came upon one woman, though, picking vegetables from her garden with great urgency. She looked up from her labor, her apron loaded with vegetables, and seemed frightened when she saw him.

”Dikembe?” she said.

“Yes,” he replied.

“He in there.” She pointed to a palm-thatched hut, the roof slanted almost to the ground on each side. She gave him a deer-in-the-headlights look, and as she ran into her home, two little girls, perhaps twins, dressed in brightly colored dresses, scampered behind her. He remembered how much Rosalee loved her garden, and he felt love and respect for the woman.

Narolie hurried around her kitchen, which was situated outside on the shady side of the house, preparing food in a frenzy. It wasn't often, actually never, that Dikembe invited white people to their home. But he loved this man, Bowman, and also felt his sorrow, which he explained was deep—so deep that even though he was silent about it, it manifested itself in his every action, and penetrated the hearts of people who were blessed and cursed with understanding. She scooted small children from under her bare feet with gentle nudges, as her oldest son, Abayomi, questioned her.

“Maman, will we eat with Father and the white man this evening?”

“No, Abay, we will eat in the kitchen, as we have practiced.”

Abayomi furrowed his brow.

“Why? Is the white man mean?”

“No!” she laughed. “Father just wants to talk man talk.”

“But I am almost a man, can I join them?”

“No, you will join me and your brothers and sisters. We are having boiled cassava, okra, and tea.”

“But why can't we eat all of this food that you are preparing?”

"Just remember, Abay, what Father Pascal taught us: Whoever has a bountiful eye will be blessed, for he shares his bread with the poor."

"Is the white man poor?" asked the boy.

Narolie swatted him on the butt.

"Gather your brothers and sisters and bring them in," she said.

As she stirred the pan of boiling manioc, she remembered what Dikembe had told her about his friend; being white, he certainly wasn't poor by their standards, but he was poverty-stricken in his heart.

Dikembe's house had once been constructed of sticks and mud, with a palm-frond roof that needed to be replaced about every two years after it had dried to a crispy tobacco color. Over the years, with the help of missionaries, European and American influence, his home had evolved into a sturdy dwelling with cinderblock walls, concrete floors, and a tin roof. But he still had a fondness for palm-frond roofs, which covered his shade room next to the house. It was his castle, providing cover from the searing sun, but allowing occasional cool breezes to flow through, solitude when he wanted to escape the riotous escapades of his many children, a place to entertain some of his colleagues without the highly spirited rascals climbing all over his guests. He could hear their laughter echoing in the house as he and Bowman enjoyed each other's company.

"They sound like they're having fun," said Bowman, as he took a sip of his vin de palme.

"Yes, they are always having fun. I hope you don't mind that we are here and they are there; they would be climbing you like a tree," laughed Dikembe.

"I wouldn't mind that at all," said Bowman, deriving great joy from the peals of squeals and laughter wafting from the house.

"They are eating in the house because some of the younger ones have not developed manners yet. But you will meet them as the night goes on; we have practiced," said Dikembe, as the lovely woman from the garden appeared with several platters and set them on the table.

Bowman stood for her, and she cast her eyes downward as Dikembe spoke.

"Mr. Bowman, this is my precious wife, Narolie," he said, and she met Bowman's eyes with hers, but only briefly.

"It's a pleasure to meet you, Narolie," said Bowman, bowing slightly, not extending his hand in respect for her shyness.

She departed quickly, as Dikembe gestured for Bowman to join him at the table.

"This is potato, beet, and broccoli salad platter. This bowl contains nshima, a tomato sauce. This platter contains a mash of cassava and corn flower, rolled into balls, we call it fufu," he said, as Narolie entered again followed by an older girl bearing other platters.

"This is lituma, a plantain dish, and moin moin, hot peppers, onions, and black-eyed peas rolled together; and loso na madeso, rice and beans," he said as Narolie and the girl swept out of the room. Lastly, he picked up a bowl and inhaled deeply of the mixture it contained. He started coughing and excused himself. Watery eyed, he gave a caveat to Bowman.

"This is a dipping sauce that you will enjoy, it is made from the piri-piri pepper, it has a wonderful aroma and taste, but, if you are not used to it, it will set you on fire for a couple of days," he laughed, as he dipped his fufu in the sauce, coughed, and attempted to grin.

"See, I am used to it," he said and offered the bowl to Bowman.

"After your warning, I will forego the hot sauce. I'd like to be able to sit down over the next few days," Bowman laughed, as Dikembe chugged his vin de palme and poured them both another.

Bowman was moved by the extravagance of the meal, knowing that Dikembe had many mouths to feed and food was not easy to come by in this part of the world, eked out of the sometimes unforgiving earth with hard labor, doled out sparingly to the lucky ones.

As they ate, Bowman mentioned Dikembe and his family's gracious hospitality.

"Dikembe, you and your family have really gone out of your way to make me feel welcome; I am honored to be your guest. Did your children partake of this meal also?"

"No, but they will make quick work of our leftovers. See that hen pecking around our garden?" he said, pointing with a plantain in his hand.

Bowman nodded.

"That is promised to them as part of Narolie's mnambe dish this weekend, and they are excited about it," said Dikembe, when a chubby little toddler waddled into the room as if on cue.

"Ah, my most recent treasure," he said as he picked her up and sat her on Bowman's lap.

"Ha! I share my treasure with you, my friend. This is Ama; it means that she was born on Saturday," he said as the child rolled contentedly in Bowman's arms, staring up at him with shining ebony eyes.

As the evening continued, each of Dikembe's children came into the room, and after they'd been introduced, the older ones cleared the table before they exited. Bowman's eyes watered as the last one passed him, carrying the bowl of piri-piri sauce.

"Would you like some more vin de palme?" said Dikembe, who was feeling the effects of the drink.

"Why not?" said Bowman, extending his cup for a refill.

Talk ran to how much the agriculture had improved in the area with the influence of people like Bowman—seeds, planting materials, fertilizers—when Dikembe changed the subject abruptly.

"Bowman, I notice how much you love children; they seem to take to you quite easily also."

"How many children do you have, Dikembe? I lost count," Bowman chuckled.

"I have eight: five with Narolie, the other three with my first wife Merveille," he said.

Bowman was intrigued, but Dikembe spared him the act of prying as he continued, his voice husky from vin de palme and sadness.

"You met two of those children this evening, the oldest. I will tell you the story if you wish."

Bowman nodded his head affirmatively.

Dikembe leaned forward in his chair, and began.

"It was during the time near the time we gained independence from the Belgian Empire. I was a member of the Alliance des Bakongo; we demanded immediate, complete independence from Belgium, and we were peaceful. Our efforts were working and we were excited about the possibility of the new Congo. At the time, I worked on the docks in Leopoldville, and Merveille worked at the Kongo Nganda, a restaurant on the harbor specializing in fish dishes with sauce and fried plantains. She was a good cook, as good as Narolie," he said quietly, gazing into the bottom of his cup.

"That week, she left our youngest children with her sister, in Katanga Province. She was allowed to bring our oldest, he was four years old, to work with her; his name was Bellande—a precious boy who behaved well," he said, filling his cup again, fuel for the continuation of his poignant tale.

"After my work was ended, I and some of my colleagues were supposed to attend a speech by representatives of Patrice Lumumba, but when we arrived at the square, we were told by well-armed gendarmerie that members of the Alliance des Bakongo were not allowed to assemble. Screaming, pushing, and shoving began as members of the BAKO and members of other factions began to scuffle, arguing about our right to assemble. At the same time, Merveille and Bellande were on the perimeter of the crowd, trying to get through to me. It got worse; shots were fired into the air, and into the crowd; thirty-four were killed that evening by the Force Publique; two of those people were my wife and son," said Dikembe as he drained the remnants of his cup.

Bowman was too stunned to offer words of condolence at first, and after a moment of silence between them he spoke.

"I am sorry, Dikembe" was all he could utter.

"I am sorry too, Bowman, I did not want to spoil this wonderful evening that I have so looked forward to," he said, shaking the calabash gourd only to find that it was empty.

"I am so blessed with a wonderful wife and family, but my sorrow continues for the loss of my loved ones."

He staggered a bit as he stood and grabbed Bowman by his arm.

"My sorrow is also for you, my friend I know you're suffering from something; I can see it in your eyes, feel it, even in the way you move, because, as I've said before, we are brothers if only in our sorrow. Believe me, I have been told of your sorrow."

"Who...who told you?" stuttered Bowman.

"The stars told me—the same stars that we are made of. Be well, Bowman, and know that I carry your burden also," he said as he walked from the shade room unsteadily.

Shocked, Bowman stood and began his walk back to the billet. He appreciated Dikembe's sincere effort to share his sorrow. And he wished he possessed the strength and character of the little man. But in his estimation, he didn't. As he passed the garden, the ill-fated hen clucked contentedly as she pecked the ground for worms and insects.

"You're the lucky one," he whispered, as he was absorbed into the darkness.

The following day, Dikembe knocked at Bowman's door around sunup. Waylaid by the amount of vin de palme from the night before, Bowman was moving slowly.

"Come in, Dikembe, and make yourself at home. I just have to finish shaving," said Bowman, lather covering one side of his face.

"Oh no, I will wait outside," said Dikembe, appearing hung over with eyeballs as red as a tomato.

"Get in here. Have a seat and relax, we're going to have a busy day digging irrigation ditches," said Bowman as he waved Dikembe in.

Dikembe was uneasy, having never been invited into a white man's home with the exception of Father Pascal, who was viewed as one of the natives. He focused on the wall at the foot of the bed at a piece of cross-stitching with the words he understood sewn in the center: "Tu es pardonné." He was making a mental note to ask Bowman about the meaning of the piece when Bowman appeared.

"Well, you ready to go?" he said, clapping his big hands together.

"I am that," said Dikembe, who decided not to invade Bowman's deep privacy with questions.

"What have you got there?" said Bowman, pointing to a sack clasped in Dikembe's work-worn hand.

"Noralie sent it for our luncheon: fufu, and a jar of piri-piri sauce for dipping," said Dikembe with a weak grin.

"Thank her for the fufu. You can drink the jar of sauce if you'd like," said Bowman as he clapped Dikembe on the back.

"Maybe we can kill some weeds with it," laughed Dikembe as they headed out the door.

Bowman made many visits to Dikembe's house following the first. He became known as Ndeko Bowman, "cousin" now, and he always brought gifts for Narolie and the children, mostly small toys—a cherished soccer ball, fruit, comic books. To Narolie's and Dikembe's dismay, the children soon forgot all manners around Ndeko, and as Dikembe feared, "climbed him like a tree." He always found time to kick the soccer ball around with the boys and to swing the jump rope for the girls. This Sunday, he gifted Narolie with a present.

"Oh Ndeko Bowman! You shouldn't have," she said, as she wrapped the beautiful floral print apron around her neck and waist. He tied the string at her back and smiled.

"A friend of mine bought the material from a catalogue, and several of the nuns, including Mother Frederika, pieced it together," he said, as she performed a little twirl to the applause of her family.

"Look, it has very big pockets for you to put the vegetables from your garden," he said, remembering Rosalee's homemade apron fitted with pockets big enough to carry potatoes, cucumbers, even small cantaloupes. He used to call it her "kangaroo" apron.

"She could even carry Ama in one of the pockets," said Dikembe, to uncontrolled laughter from his offspring.

"Ndeko Bowman. Please come more often," requested Narolie, who usually deferred to Dikembe for the honor of asking, but she forgot her manners in her joy and affection for Bowman.

"I'll try. But I don't want to wear out my welcome. As a matter of fact, I must go now," he said as the children whined.

"Come back again," said Dikembe as all of the children walked Ndeko Bowman to the road.

Chapter 21

CONFESSIONS OF THE SILENT MAN

Bowman slogged through the ankle-deep mud and water, setting seedlings. It was backbreaking work, made palatable by the sweet singing of the uncomplaining women of the village as they planted the rice. Weeks earlier, he and the men followed his crop irrigation scheme, damming a portion of the river and channeling the water into a low-lying field that had been slashed and burned to make the soil more fruitful. From his studies, the harvest of rice would handily exceed the nutrients formerly provided to the villagers by millet, sorghum, and other cereals. He was comparing this grueling work to the ease of farming in Tennessee, with modern tools, when his reverie was interrupted.

"Homme Muette, there are mosquitoes circling your head, they are going to carry you away," said a cheerful voice behind him. Bowman wasn't insulted by being called "The Silent Man," knowing that it wasn't meant to be an insult. The buoyant voice was Belvie's—a statuesque, heavy-boned young mother from the village. Her son, Gloire, snoozed away comfortably, strapped to her back in a colorful baby sling.

"They are everywhere. Are they biting you or Gloire, Belvie?"

"No, they are not. Maybe because our black skin is not as inviting as yours," she said as she hiked up her long skirt and re-knotted it between her legs.

"I would say that it is because your skin is superior to mine," he said, and Belvie laughed, along with the other women, proud of the compliment. They were also happy that they had squeezed some words out of "Homme Muette"—a man they had come to love and respect, the man whose silence reflected the pain that many of them identified as their own. In addition, since his visit to Dikembe's home, once-shy villagers seemed more open with him.

Although Bowman had applied copious amounts of cream and spray, they failed to deter the mosquitoes that feasted on his blood, making the work more miserable than it should be. And he wasn't concerned about malaria because he'd taken the proper steps to prevent that dilemma before coming to Africa—or so he thought.

It was unfortunate that "The Silent Man" imprisoned his feelings inwardly, because he failed to complain when he first began having symptoms: high fever, chills, muscle pain. He disguised these symptoms very well, remaining to himself, which was accepted as normal for him. When he didn't show up for breakfast one morning, Catrin and Dikembe went to his billet to find him shaking in his bed, covered with several blankets. Soon, he was surrounded by other doctors, nuns, and researchers, who took his blood in greater but less malevolent quantities than the female Anopheles gambiae mosquito that infected him.

On testing his blood, it was found that he had malaria parasites in his liver, which were resistant to the medications he had taken.

"It looks like Plasmodium falciparum, but we can fix that," said Catrin, who, along with her colleagues, concocted a powerful cocktail of anti-malarial medications to combat the problem. Bowman, however, had a long journey ahead of him before he was cured.

They'd moved him to the clinic where he could be monitored more efficiently. This evening, it was Catrin's turn to be near his bedside, although she was there at other times to minister to his needs. She was worried because his fever was raging, and periodically, he was moaning incomprehensively. Her heart broke for him, knowing that this proud man would hate for others to see him in this helpless state.

A strong thunderstorm was raging, pounding the tin roof,

sounding like thunderous applause as strobes of blue lightning followed by cannon shots of thunder illuminated the interior of the clinic. He shouted above the dissonance in a tortured voice.

"Rosalee! Is the storm bothering you? Come here, honey, and I'll hold you to sleep." He reached into the air and waved his hand.

"Durand, Durand, hop in bed with Mamma and Daddy," he yelled as another crashing boom shook the little building.

He curled his arms against his chest, as if he were holding someone tightly.

"I'm sorry! I'm sorry that Bernard killed you! Please, please forgive me! I am so sorry, Armandus," he sobbed.

Catrin stopped dabbing at his forehead, intrigued by the name he uttered. She remembered the tales that Christophe and his family had told her of the Allied soldier who had mistakenly killed Armandus.

She felt guilty for probing into Bowman's tortured psyche, but queried him anyway.

"Armandus? Where did Armandus live?" she asked with urgency in her voice.

"Ardennes… St. Vith," he whispered, as if to keep a secret.

The following clap of thunder felt as if it emanated from her soul.

She knelt by his bedside, and lay her head on his sweaty chest.

"Bowman…Bowman…you poor creature," she sobbed.

He wrapped his arm around her neck.

"Go to sleep, Rosalee. It's alright, baby," he said comfortingly.

"Bowman, Bowman, I am so sorry," she cried.

"Tu es pardonné," he said, patting her back gently.

The storm subsided at dawn, along with Bowman's rampant fever. Thanks to quinine and antibiotics and Catrin's compassionate, professional attention, Bowman was sleeping soundly now. Exhausted, she stroked his hair and smoothed his face, suspecting that their relationship had been preordained for the answers to many questions.

As he recuperated, he was moved back to his billet to make room for other patients at the clinic. He was visited several times daily by the villagers, nuns, and his colleagues.

He flinched as Catrin took a blood sample.

"These have been getting better. I think you have, how you say, 'whipped this thing,'" she said, but as usual, he was unsmiling at the news.

"I was out of my head there for a while, wasn't I?"

"Pretty much so," she said as she packed up her medical supplies.

"Did a lot of people hear me?"

"No, just me."

She answered him with honesty and factually, as if she had taken notes.

"You talked about Durand, Rosalee, Bernard, and Armandus."

"Armandus? What did I say?"

"You asked him to forgive you."

She wanted to say more about her relationship to Armandus' family, but decided not to, fearing that information would hinder their rapport.

Bowman spoke in a whisper.

"He forgave me."

"Then feel blessed and accept his forgiveness," she said.

"I will when I feel that I can repay him," he said, pointing to the cross-stitch hanging on the wall at the foot of his bed.

"I'd like for you to do me a favor, Catrin. If something ever happens to me, I'd like for you to ensure that that cross-stitch ends up in the hands of my brother, Bernard."

"Does that mean you forgive him? Why don't you tell him yourself?"

"I plan on it. But I'd feel better if I have a contingency plan, okay?"

"Okay," she said as she left.

There was no response because he was asleep—peacefully.

She delighted in watching him gain strength. It seemed that some of his sadness had dissipated along with the parasites in his body. He laughed now occasionally, much to the enjoyment of Dikembe and Belvie, who never missed a chance to joke with him; the nuns, who recognized his specialness and loved him for it; and all of his colleagues who were bolstered in spirit by his recovery. Catrin was aware of an aura of sadness that lingered around him, but, to the astute observer that sadness was evident in everyone, including herself. She began making plans to eradicate some of her sadness, realizing that it was her responsibility to initiate that mending many years ago.

Sitting on the hillside in the evening, after work in the fields had become a ritual for Bowman and Dikembe, their talks had become more interesting now that Dikembe had shared his story.

Bowman enjoyed the antics of Dikembe's two small sons as they wrestled like frisky lion cubs, tumbling down the grassy slope.

"You are blessed to have your children so close by," said Bowman, as the little fellows squealed and hollered.

"Yes, but they will leave someday. What is your son's name?"

"Durand."

"I am sorry that he is so far away, brother," said Dikembe, placing his leathery hand on Bowman's shoulder.

"We will be reunited, hopefully soon," said Bowman, who laughed as the boys cascaded into his lap.

Gossip about Bowman and other white people was a strong thread in the fabric of village life—as strong as Dikembe's intuition and his faith in the stars. But he still wondered if Bowman was still hallucinating from his bout with malaria.

Bowman was still weak from his ordeal, and alternated days in the field with days assisting in the clinic.

"Thank you for helping today, we are always shorthanded around here," said Mother Frederika.

"It's my pleasure," said Bowman, as he organized bandages and medications on a shelf.

"Are you getting stronger, Bowman? I have been praying for you and so have many others."

Bowman turned and spoke earnestly.

"Your prayers worked, Mother, for I am healing physically, but I need to regain the grace of God lost through my sins," he said as they both sat down on a bench near the shelf.

"Are you religious?" she asked, interested in his remark.

"I was Sunday school superintendent at Harrogate Baptist Church once, some time ago." He smiled.

"Oh, I was going to suggest that you confess your sins to Father Pascal. But you are not Catholic. As you know, we believe that a priest is an intermediary for God. He has the authority to forgive sins."

Bowman shook his head.

"I respect that, but I have been taught that sins are forgiven alone, through faith in Christ."

"I respect that too. But if it will help, I will listen to your troubles if you think it will lessen the sorrow of your soul," she said, touching his arm gently.

Her heart broke as he told his story. She had heard some of the story before, but was unaware that he was unburdening his soul in preparation for the reunion.

⟡

As he talked, he remembered some of the bizarre scenarios that comprised the wacked-out hallucinations that occurred during his raging fevers. He focused especially on the one that replayed most often.

He was walking around the compound, sloshing through a river of blood. There was fire all around him, and the blood felt hot on his ankles. He came to the river, and to his gladness, there stood Rosalee and Durand, their arms outstretched in greeting. He rushed to them but they held their palms up in a "stop" motion.

"Not yet!" they cried in unison. Rosalee rushed to him, fluttering around him like a butterfly, straightening his clothing, brushing ashes off his shoulders.

Durand clapped his hands together.

"It's almost over!" he said joyfully.

"Yes, and it's almost the beginning," Rosalee added.

Suddenly, he could feel the river of blood retreating at his feet and the surrounding fires were extinguished, hissing and spitting as they died out.

"Go on, Bowman, and finish this," said Rosalee as Durand grabbed her hand.

"I will," said Bowman, ecstatic at the thought. They waved gaily to him as if he were going on a day trip. Armandus appeared in the roadway, reached into his back pocket and produced the cross-stitch, and handed it to Durand. Durand ran to his father, and Bowman longed to pick him up and hold him forever. But somehow, he was aware of the rules; he knew that at this moment, he was denied that privilege. He had to "finish it" before realizing his most ardent wish.

"Make sure Uncle Bernard gets this," said Durand, placing the cross-stitch into his hands.

"I've taken care of that already, Son. Wait for me, please."

"We will," they said in perfect unison.

He turned and walked slowly back to the village, sidestepping mounds of smoldering ruins.

As he passed his billet, Catrin appeared at the door.

"Do you have it?" she said.

He did not reply as he placed the cross-stitch in her hand. He was tired to the point of exhaustion, but he kept moving forward, eager to "finish it."

He was actually sweating after confiding his story to Mother Frederika, and she dabbed at his forehead with a handkerchief.

After hearing the tortured tale from his lips, she was concerned that he was contemplating suicide.

"Are you eager to 'finish it,' my dear?" she said, pitying his angst-ridden soul.

"I don't know exactly what 'finish it' means," he said, his hand trembling as he wiped sweat from his brow.

"All I can say is that suicide is not an answer to your dilemma."

He laughed as he lied.

"The thought never entered my mind. But I do know that my Creator will provide the answers to all of my questions someday," he said, as he rose slowly from the bench. He wobbled a bit and leaned against the wall for support as Mother Frederika came to him.

"Why don't you lie down for a while? We have room in the clinic, and I'll look after you."

"No thank you, Mother, but with your blessing I will knock off for today and go back to my billet. I could get some rest, for I have plans for this evening," he said.

"Fine, but let me get someone to walk you back to your billet," she said.

"Thank you. Will you please not tell anyone about our conversation today?"

"You have my promise," she said as she hugged him.

It was delightfully cool in his room, and the whirring of the ceiling fan was hypnotic, his eyelids drooped heavily . He closed all of the blinds, and the dark, soothing to his aching head, enticed him to cool sheets and blessed unconsciousness—an opportunity to sleep, hopefully a dreamless sleep, to banish his sorrow for a time and to distill his exhaustion. But he was slapped by his mind, which shouted at him, "Sleep must wait until you prepare for this evening."

He retrieved his suitcase from the closet and laid it on his bed. Next, he opened the drawer to his nightstand and dumped the contents on the bed also. He rummaged through the items in the suitcase and from the nightstand, and placed them in a bag that he was going to use to collect plant samples.

"There," he said satisfactorily, as he glanced at his alarm clock.

"Hey! I have almost four hours to go. I can get a couple of hours' sleep before it's time," he said aloud.

He replaced the suitcase and the nightstand drawer in their proper places, set the alarm clock, and fell into bed, racing to the solace of deep slumber.

Chapter 22

SOWING BOUNTIFULLY

It was after supper and Ndeko Bowman had distributed knickknacks and doodads to the children, and he and Dikembe sat in the shade room enjoying one another's company.

"Ndeko Bowman, it seems that you are gaining strength after your peril," said Dikembe as he lit his pipe.

"I'm feeling better every day, but I am not allowed any vin de palme for a while," he said.

"That is good, it will keep me from drinking it," laughed Dikembe, remembering the hangover he suffered from one night of imbibing with Bowman.

They were silent for a while, listening to the laughter of children in the distance blended with the oncoming of the night chorus of amphibians and insects.

"Ndeko Bowman, I hesitate to ask this because it is a sad thought for me and my family. When is it you have to leave us?"

Bowman reached beside his chair and placed a sack in his lap—a prelude to answering the question.

"I will be sad too. A couple more months and I will be heading back home, my brother. That's why I wanted to give you some small things that signify my feelings for you, Narolie, and your family—my nieces and nephews," he said, reaching into the bag.

"I have to be honest. I'm trying to whittle down my possessions so I don't have so much to take back with me," he laughed, as he pulled out a couple of dog-eared books.

"This is a book I think you will enjoy and learn from on organic farming; it might help with your garden plot at home as well as some of the projects we've been working on," he said.

"Ooh, thank you, Ndeko Bowman," he said, rubbing the cover of the well-thumbed book as if it were a magic lamp.

Bowman extracted another book from the bag.

"This is a book called *Silent Spring*. It's about how pesticides and chemicals we use on plants are destroying our earth."

"That is why we plant our maize with molasses grass, yes?"

"Yes," said Bowman as he reached further into the bag and brought forth a small Bible, also well-thumbed.

"This is for Narolie. It is my wife's. Like Narolie, she is a good wife and gardener. I have marked a verse with the bookmark that Narolie will like," he said, handing the book to Dikembe, who received the gift reverently. He turned to the marked passage and read aloud.

2 Corinthians 9:6: "Now, I say, he who sows sparingly will also reap sparingly, and he who sows bountifully, will also reap bountifully."

"That makes a lot of sense, doesn't it," said Bowman, still searching for other objects in the bag.

"And this is for you, even though I've never had to worry about you being late for work."

Dikembe opened the small box and gasped as he pulled the gold pocket watch out and unraveled the chain.

"It was my father's watch and he left it to me."

"But wouldn't you rather leave it to someone in your family?"

"You, Narolie, and the children are my family in Africa, and I want you to have something to remember me by. I have a brother in America, and I will leave much to him," said Bowman, as he stood and extracted an envelope from the nearly empty bag.

"And lastly, I have a gift for you, Narolie, and the children, in hopes that it will be used wisely to make all of your lives better," said Bowman, and he tossed the envelope to Dikembe as he headed out the opening of the shade room.

Dikembe was seated at the table in a state of shock when Narolie entered the shade room.

"Was it a good visit with Ndeko, Husband?"

She became concerned when he didn't answer her. Instead, he handed her the envelope as if it were a foreclosure notice on their home.

She hesitated to look inside, and shrieked when she beheld the contents. She hastily closed the envelope when her oldest daughter came running into the room.

"Is something wrong, Maman?" she asked concernedly, and Dikembe answered.

"A bug just crawled across Maman's foot," he laughed. "Now go to bed, Daughter."

When the girl left the room, Narolie seated herself on the bench next to Dikembe, and both of them had a difficult time refraining from shouting as they counted the money.

"Over eleven hundred American dollars!" she whispered incredulously.

"Eleven hundred and twenty-eight to be exact," he answered, also in a whisper.

They hastily counted the money again, converting the bounty in their minds to francs Congolais.

Catrin had just finished her second shower of the day, and was readying herself for bed, when the knock came at her door.

"Just a minute," she said, wondering who could be calling at this late hour.

"It's me, the recipient of the ice-pick award, and a liver full of malaria," said Bowman.

She opened the door, happy to see him.

"What in the world do you want at this time of night?" she asked as he came in.

"I have a present for you," he said, handing her an object wrapped in burlap.

"Oh, Bowman, what is it?"

"It's a picture of us."

"I don't remember a picture of us."

"You forget so easily," he said, as he grabbed her around her waist and pulled her to him.

"I hope I will be forgiven for this," he said, as he kissed her hard on the mouth—once, twice, three times, like a thirsty man gulping water.

He released her gently, and touched her face.

"Thank you, Catrin," he said, and he disappeared into the night.

It took her a while to get over the experience, and when she found the strength, she unwrapped the burlap wrapping.

The photo featured a proud, smiling Bowman, an angelic-looking woman, and a precious little boy.

There was a note attached that said, *Remember me, as I remember you.*

She held the photo to her breast, and cried herself to sleep.

He awoke the next morning amazingly refreshed, unburdened. He reached into the drawer of the bedside table to get the small Bible, and smiled, remembering that he had given it to Narolie.

"Hell, she'll make better use of it than I have," he said, glancing at the cross-stitch on the wall at the foot of his bed.

"Besides, thanks to you, St. Rosalie, this is the only inspiration I need," he said, smoothing out the cloth lovingly.

As he walked to the clinic, he thought of his romantic encounter with Rosalee the night before; he envisioned holding her again to-night, and forever.

"One more day," he said, as he quickened his step toward providence.

Chapter 23

MBOKU AND THE SIMBAS

Catrin was moving slowly, having not slept well the night before. Bowman's visit had pleased her, but she was unnerved just the same, fearing the consequences of his fragile mental state. She had the uncanny feeling that he was experiencing a premonition, or was orchestrating his demise. The air was sluggish that morning as she and Father Pascal loaded the Jeep for a day trip to Owandi.

"We should be back well before evening," said Father Pascal as he slid a box of syringes into the back of the WWII vintage vehicle.

"I'm a bit nervous. There is rumor of MPR activity in the area," said Catrin in the midst of a huge yawn.

"Mouvement Populaire de la Revolution holds no threat to us, as long as we adopt African names," laughed Father Pascal.

"We'd better dye our skin black while we're at it," said Catrin, and the Jeep made a popping, spitting sound as they sputtered off down the dusty road. Mboku spied their departure through his binoculars.

Mboku was a Congolese Maoist Rebel who followed the tenets of Pierre Mulele, who was loyal to Premier Patrice Lumumba. The current president, Joseph Mobutu, orchestrated the executions of both men. Mboku hated Mobutu with a passion, and led a small band of rebels in cross-border insurgencies against government forces, and raids on helpless villages for no evident purpose other than to spread terror and his personal loathing for the government. His hate ran deep, especially for the village in which he was raised. He considered the residents to be sheep that allowed his enemy, Mobutu, and whites to debase them and dishonor their culture. He would rather see them dead than to kowtow to their masters. As time moved on, he rejected some of his Maoist codes of belief, introducing savagery as a major component of his evil routine.

It was noon, and Mboku and his men, high on hemp and blood-lust, crouched in a shady alcove just outside of the village of Yamboki, Mboku's village. Despite the shade, the heat, and the absence of moving air was stifling. They brandished an eclectic assortment of weapons: spears, long knives, and machetes, and some relatively modern rifles and pistols. Mboku carried a prestigious Sten Gun, which was capable of cutting a person in half—and he had proudly accomplished that act many times.

"We will divide into two squads. The first squad will round up all of the villagers and assemble them in the marketplace. If you wish, you may order all of the female prisoners to disrobe. You may do with the female prisoners as you like, and that includes the nuns."

His men smiled at the thought.

"If the men, especially the priests, and other white men do not cooperate, cut off their beards and slice their throats. The second squad, led by me, will attack the hospital, and we will take supplies and prisoners from there," he said as he waved them onward.

Dikembe and Narolie were ecstatic with their gifts from Bowman and looked forward to thanking him profusely for their good fortune. They sat in the shade room talking of the bright future for their family when they heard mean shouting emanating from the nearby jungle, and cries coming from the homes of their neighbors. Dikembe peered through a slit in the palm fronds of his shade-room roof and spied several freakish-looking Simbas slinking on the perimeter of the village. He ran to Narolie, wild-eyed and frantic.

"Run! Gather the children and hide them in the cave in the hill behind the garden," he said, nudging her forward.

"Come, join us, Husband," she said, taking his hand in hers.

The entire village had not been alerted of the invasion, only the villagers on the outskirts, who were rounded up and threatened with death or worse if they cried out. Those who tried to hide were beaten unmercifully by the Simbas, and the invaders were thorough in their searches. Mboku, knowing the lay of the land and most of the villagers, was most thorough, and he yelled with glee, like a child on an Easter egg hunt, when he ferreted out a person or a family from their hiding places.

"I knew you would be hiding there, old man! I remember when your son would hide from me in that place when we were children, playing 'Hide from the Lion,'" he would shout merrily, smacking and punching the old fellow about the head and shoulders.

They moved stealthily from house to house, searching the gardens and perimeters. As they were searching Dikembe's house and shade room, Mboku strayed to the hill where he played as a child, knowing that beneath the hill was a small cave. Other Simbas started to follow him, and he motioned them forward with a hand signal.

Dikembe, Narolie, and their clan cowered as far back in the cave as possible. They were quaking with fear, and frantic that little Ama would cry out. The children took turns comforting her, as Narolie and Dikembe listened as close to the entrance to the cave as possible. They heard crackling of the dry underbrush outside of the cave, and ran to their children with their index fingers to their lips.

They bunched up as close as they could to one another, when Ama started to cry. They were trying to calm her when a voice spoke from the cave entrance.

"Shut her up or you will all die," said Mboku as he appeared threateningly before them. All of the children began whimpering at his fierce appearance.

"I said 'shut up'!" he whispered in an angry rasp, waving his machete menacingly.

"Mboku, it is me, Dikembe," said Dikembe as he stepped forward haltingly.

"Ha! I knew that you would choose this place where we would play as children. I knew this is where the sheep would lead their lambs to cower in the darkness," said Mboku, unsmiling.

"Yes, these precious ones are our children. Do you have children?" said Narobie, hoping to calm him, and respect the innocence of the little ones.

"I have children in Gabon, Cameroon, Angola, and Republique du Congo. They are not sheep to be herded in a cave, to die in the darkness. They adhere to the doctrine of our murdered leaders Pierre Mulele and Patrice Lumumba, and they live to destroy Mobutu, the coward and ruination of our country," said Mboku, obviously unstable, high on khat or a combination of other drugs, with a fierce stare and spittle flying from his mouth as he voiced his rhetoric.

"Mboku, the Simbas were defeated by the ANC many years ago. Why do you continue to fight, when you don't have to?" said Dikembe, who stepped back hastily as Mboku charged him like an elephant, stopping just inches from his face.

"I fight to honor the men who gave us independence from Belgium; I fight to kill the white witches who were involved in their deaths: the Belge, Britons, and the United States. And I will kill all of those sheep who now bow to Mobutu," said Mboku, as he sheathed his machete and un-shouldered his Sten Gun.

The children whimpered as Narolie and Dikembe fell to their knees.

"Please, take us hostage, kill us, but allow our children to live," pleaded Dikembe.

"You are not as brave, Mr. Sheep, as you were when we were children," sneered Mboku. Then he hesitated as a thought occurred to him.

"Where is that scar from the knife—on your arm, or on your back?"

"My arm," said Dikembe, rolling up his shirt sleeve to display a raised scar about six inches in length.

"Why did you try to take that knife from that drunken man, who was trying to stab me?"

"Because I loved you, Mboku. I still love you," said Dikembe.

For a brief moment, Mboku dropped any semblance of bravado, even hate, and his expression spoke: *How could you love a person like me?*

"You are my brother; my flesh and bone," said Dikembe, as if he could read his mind. Mboku looked at him incredulously. The hatred returned to his face.

"You are a sheep, and I despise you," spat Mboku as he turned to walk away. He was just a silhouette in the light of the cave entrance when he turned and spoke again.

"Stay here, sheep. And don't bleat until darkness returns."

Bowman was assisting Mother Frederika and Sister Cecelia with feeding a malaria victim when the first shouts, screams, and gunfire reached their ears. He raced to the window to see villagers being herded into the streets by terrorists, who grinned in enjoyment of the tumult and horror they were dispensing.

"Dikembe, Narolie, the children; I have to go to them," said Bowman, dashing for the door.

"No, Bowman. You are weak and you are needed here; you will be cut down or captured," said Mother Frederika as she barred the door with her body. She was almost knocked off her feet as the door burst open.

Mboku and his Simbas, coal-black and glistening with sweat and blood, some attired in leopard skins, manes of monkey fur, and feathers, others in fatigues, burst into the infirmary.

"Who is in charge here?" he screamed, as his men pointed their automatic weapons, spears, and machetes at the helpless patients and the few nuns attending them. Bowman started to speak, but Mother Frederika beat him to the punch.

"God is in charge here, sir, and He wants you to leave."

A sardonic smirk on his face, Mboku related Mother Frederika's answer to his soldiers, who laughed raucously, hurling obscenities at no one in particular as Mboku strutted around the room, staring menacingly at those who bravely returned his nasty gape.

"You are incorrect, Nun. It is I who is in charge here and I do not want to leave, just yet," yelled Mboku as he sidled up to Bowman.

"Is this man one of your priests?"

"No, but he is a child of God, just as you are, with several exceptions," said Mother Frederika, stepping protectively in front of Bowman.

"And what are those exceptions?" sneered Mboku, leaning close to Frederika's ear.

"He is dedicated to the service of your people instead of destroying them."

"Ha! Tell me of another exception."

"He is not a coward," said Mother Frederika, as members of Mboku's cadre gasped at her insolence.

The attending sisters screamed and the soldiers chortled as Mboku struck down Mother Frederika with his machete.

"You son of a bitch!" screamed Bowman as he attempted to snatch the machete from Mboku's hands. He was succeeding in overpowering his adversary when one of the Simbas impaled him with a short spear. Bowman fell over the body of Mother Frederika.

Mboku, excited by the horror, bent very close to Bowman's tortured face as he writhed on the floor.

"So, he is not a coward, eh? Are you a coward? Then what do you say before I cut out your liver and eat it as you die, hero?" Bowman whispered something.

"What is it he says?"

One of the nuns translated Bowman's words.

"He says, 'You would not like my liver; but thank you for ending my misery,'" replied the trembling nun.

Perplexed, Mboku paused for a moment to digest the remark. Then he smiled, which seemed unnatural—more like a grimace.

"Thank you? Then that makes what I am about to do more pleasurable," said Mboku, as he turned and swung his machete heavily at Bowman's neck.

Mboku enjoyed the graphic outpouring of grief in the room. He allowed the screaming and sobbing to continue for a while, ordering his men to scour the medicine cabinets. When that was done, he gave a nod to his soldiers, who aimed their weapons at the pitiful little group and awaited his signal to fire. Some of the nuns began to pray aloud.

"Go ahead and say your prayers, Christian people. But don't pray for me and my comrades. We have been forgiven by your hero," said Mboku, and his followers laughed as he wiped his bloody machete on Bowman's and Mother Frederika's bodies.

"But his forgiveness of me has not saved your miserable lives today. Nuns, disrobe for the pleasure of my warriors," ordered Mboku. Suddenly, the roar of airplane engines was heard, and a sentry appeared, yelling and pointing skyward. Mboku barked an order; the soldiers gripped their weapons and followed him briskly out of the door. As the cowards abandoned their horrific agenda, gunfire and frantic yelling was heard as they scattered like marauding baboons into the bush.

Chapter 24

THE QUICK DEPARTURE

Catrin and Father Pascal heard the gunfire too, and the drone of planes, as they pulled out onto the main road.

"Look!" said Father Pascal, gesturing towards the sky as parachutes drifted toward the earth.

They drove slowly, tentatively, unable to confirm what was happening. Suddenly, a group of uniformed white men emerged from the jungle, their weapons pointed menacingly at them. Father Pascal attempted to back up, but one of the men fired his weapon in the air, and the Jeep came to a jolting halt. The men stood, spraddle-legged, their weapons at the ready as one of them, broad shouldered and heavy-chested, approached them.

"Are you Father Pascal and Dr. de Jonge? If so, I need to see your identification," he said in French.

"Yes, and who are you?" said Father Pascal haltingly.

"I am Captain Goossens, and we are of the Belgian Para-Commandos," he said briskly. As he leafed through the identification papers, Catrin studied the phrase embroidered above his fatigue pocket: *Nee Lactania Nee Metu* ("Neither boasting nor fearing").

"What is happening, Captain?" Catrin asked fearfully. She took a sharp breath at his answer.

"Rebels have attacked the village of Yamboki. We got word of their plans and we are clearing them out now," he said as his radio crackled.

Before the pair had a chance to ask more questions, the captain ordered Father Pascal into the backseat.

"I will drive. I am told that it is safe to approach," he said, as he shifted the vehicle heavily into gear.

As they entered the village, the only sounds were of moaning and crying. Bodies were strewn about the square like jackstraws—some writhing in pain, others still as statues; the metallic smell of blood filled the air.

Catrin and Father Pascal prepared to leap out of the Jeep, but Goossens stopped them. Father Pascal implored him.

"I must administer last rites, please, let me go to them," he cried.

"I am sorry. First, we have to determine if the bodies of the wounded and the dead have not been mined. It won't take long," he said as he pulled up in front of the hospital.

Catrin was aghast at the scene in the clinic: medicine cabinets sacked, equipment overturned, and the floor slick with the blood from the fatal wounds of Mother Frederika, who appeared to be peacefully sleeping, and Bowman, his neck bearing a hideous gash, his face contorted in an agonized death grimace, a spear impaled just below his heart.

As the wounded and the dead were carried into the makeshift morgue, Catrin continued to cradle Bowman's head in her arms, as Father Pascal ministered tenderly to the still form of Mother Frederika.

"We have many wounded to tend to, and I have been given permission to administer last rites," said Father Pascal, rising, extending his hands to assist Catrin to her feet.

Catrin released her hold on Bowman and rested his head gently on the floor. She kissed his forehead—a lengthy kiss meant for a child.

"I must go, mon ange," she said softly, and covered his mutilated neck with a towel as she rose from his body.

Catrin moved zombie-like as she packed up her belongings. The Para-Commandos gave her and her colleagues just a day to ready themselves for the trip home. She willed herself to go to Bowman's quarters and pack what little belongings he had to take with her. One item she was dedicated to retrieving was the cross-stitch scene hanging on the wall at the foot of his bunk.

Father Pascal, normally a study in spiritual strength, had great difficulty leading the mass for Mother Frederika. With his back turned to the congregation, he cried as her scapular was placed over her head and the casket was closed.

He led the phalanx of nuns, volunteers, and villagers to the cemetery in a procession bearing the caskets of Mother Frederika and Bowman Rafferty. The nuns lent decorum to the ceremony, chanting the *Liberia*, an ancient prayer for the dead. At the gravesites, Father Pascal did his priestly duty, offering the homily and all of the proper prayers. Then, he opened up a book to read a beautiful prayer by Father Bede Jarrett. The nuns' lips moved in silent prayer as he read:

"We seem to give them back to you, O God, who gave them to us. Yet as you did not lose them in giving, so we do not lose them by their return. Not as the world gives do you give, O Lover of souls. What you give you take not away, for what is yours is ours also if we are yours. And life is eternal, and love is immortal, and death is only an horizon, and an horizon is nothing, save the limit of our sight. Lift us up, strong Son of God, that we may see further; cleanse our eyes that we may see more clearly; draw us closer to yourself that we may know ourselves to be nearer our loved ones who are with you. And while you do prepare a place for us, prepare us also for that happy place, that where you are, we may be also for evermore."

As the nuns and some of the crowd retreated down the hillside, Father Pascal knelt by the grave of his great friend.

"Mother Frederika, I will never forget our wonderful friendship, and the great deeds you have done in your life, especially on this, your beloved, continent. You will be in my prayers daily, and I look forward to being with you and our Savior," he said, as he rose and made his way to Catrin.

Catrin stood on the hillside overlooking the river where she and Bowman had swum together as Dikembe's family mourned loudly. Dikembe and Abaya hammered rough crosses into the fresh red soil at the gravesite, and when they had finished Dikembe looked at Catrin sorrowfully; his eyes were red and filled with tears. When Father Pascal had finished with his words, Dikembe said nothing, deferring to Narolie, who was wearing her new apron. She nodded her head solemnly, and one by one, the children placed a flower on Ndeko Bowman's grave. Dikembe and Narolie, hand in hand, were the last to perform the honor.

"We will remember you, Ndeko Bowman; your silent kindness and your love for little children. Be at peace now, Ndeko Bowman, as you cradle your child and your woman in the afterlife," said Dikembe, and as they had practiced, he and his family turned as one and walked slowly down the hill from the gravesites. Dikembe motioned for his family to stop, as he pulled the watch from his deep shirt pocket. As he held it in his hand, each family member touched it reverently—a remembrance of the cherished legacy of Ndeko Bowman.

Catrin watched them, and loved them, as Bowman loved them. She turned and spoke to him. "Cradle your loved ones, Bowman… hold them in your strong arms, and never let them go," she said, sniffling as the hot wind sifted through her hair, and red dust devils swirled about her feet. She knelt and kissed the cross.

"I will carry out your request, Bowman, Thank you for saving me," she whispered, as Father Pascal led her to the Land Rover.

The power was out at the hotel as usual, and the temperature was so hot at noonday that even Roger (whose new African name was Masimbwa) was perspiring. He stood in the doorway of the former Royal Leopoldville, which was now called "The Royal Kinshasa" at the command of Premier Joseph Mobutu, who insisted that the names and places of his country be absolutely African. Mobutu followed his own directive, changing his name to "Mobutu sese seko Kuku Ngbendu waza Banga": "The all-powerful warrior who, because of his endurance and inflexible will to win, will go from conquest to conquest, leaving fire in his wake."

Masimbwa shielded his eyes with his hand, noticing a column of dust which rose in the distance amidst the whine and rumble of heavy vehicles.

The travelers in the caravan of mostly military vehicles were relieved to arrive at the airport, where C-130 transports sat on the runway waiting to take them home.

As the ragtag survivors, mostly white-skinned, boarded the planes, many wondered fearfully what was to happen to the people they had come to love back in Yamboki and elsewhere.

"My dear, I am so sorry it had to end like this," said Father Pascal to Catrin, holding her face in his hands.

"Oh, Father. I can only thank God for having known you, Mother Frederika, Bowman Rafferty, and all of those who suffered under the hands of those monsters, whom I shall never forget either," she said, as the big engines whined and propellers began to turn slowly in the thick air.

A paratrooper approached Catrin.

"You must go, mademoiselle, the doors are closing," he said, gently pulling at her arm.

"I love you, Father!" she cried, as the roar increased in intensity.

He made the sign of the cross.

"Forgive them; forgive them," he yelled back, but his words were obliterated by the bellow of the engines as the plane taxied down the runway.

BOOK 5

HOMEWARD BOUND

Chapter 25

THE WISDOM OF GUILLAUME

Margot was saddened that her mother would be absent for such a long time, but she was ecstatic that she would be staying with her cousins near St. Vith for nearly the entire summer.

"Pappa, you must have had fun growing up here in the Ardennes," she said as they sped along the twisting roads outside of St. Vith in his Porsche.

Christophe laughed.

"Well, we had fun when we weren't working, but that was most of the time. Farm life was hard, but it had its rewards," he said, as they slowed to a stop to allow a herd of sheep to cross the road.

"Was it harder than what you do now?"

"Physically, it was. But it was simpler; you didn't have to worry about someone playing mind games with you. You didn't have to be concerned about people lying to you," he said, as the shepherd prodded the last ewe across the road with his cane. At those words, the image of the love of his life flashed across his mind. It shattered into fragments as she spoke the words, "je t'adore," and he felt bereaved at his loss—more so than if it had been a death. He raised his sunglasses and pinched the bridge of his nose at the center of his eyes.

"You can go now, Pappa," said Margot, eager to arrive at their destination.

"Sorry. Just a little headache," he said and gunned the engine.

The girls flew down the hill to greet them, and Margot was out of the car before it stopped rolling. The country girls and their city cousin learned much from one another during their summer visits, and always looked forward to these reunions.

"Manon, Justine!" she cried as they fell into each other's arms with the heartfelt zeal inherent to their gender.

"Come, look what we have!" they cried, and the sisters grabbed Margot's hand as they raced toward the barn.

Christophe strolled toward the house, where Jolien and Uncle Guillaume waited for him on the porch. From first observation, he noticed that Jolien had chunked up a bit with age, and Uncle Guillaume, ancient now, was ensconced in a wheelchair. Although it was warm, he had a shawl draped around his shoulders.

"Welcome, Christophe!" said Jolien, wrapping her arms around him. Uncle Guillaume said nothing, but stretched his liver-spotted hand out to hold Christophe's hand weakly.

"That stroke he suffered about four months ago took a lot out of him, didn't it, Uncle Guillaume?" said Jolien, smoothing the old man's hair down.

Christophe studied the old fellow with a practiced eye.

"Are you able to talk, Uncle?" he said in a loud voice.

"Yes…but not much," whispered the old man, still clinging to Christophe with his cold claw of a hand.

"Well, I plan on staying a few days if you don't mind, and we'll talk of old times, and I'll do all of the talking if you don't feel like it," said Christophe, and he kissed the old fellow on the cheek as he stood. The gesture pleased Guillaume, and his eyes watered as he spoke.

"Adelheide's boy, where's your girlfriend?"

Jolien laughed.

"You mean his wife, Catrin? She's in Africa."

Guillaume looked confused.

"Why would she be there?" he said, voice trembling from age and his affliction.

"I'm not sure," said Christophe sadly.

When Uncle Guillaume had become too decrepit to take care of the large house, Jolien, her daughter Morgane, and Morgane's daughters Manon and Justine moved in after selling Jolien's grandmother's small home up the road.

"Morgane works at a bakery in St. Vith, and we get along just fine with her support, the money we received from Grandmother's farm, and monetary help from you, Uncle Guillaume, and Matthias' insurance," she said as she brought him another beer from the refrigerator.

"If you require more, I will be happy to increase the payments."

"No, no. What you give is more than we need; and we thank you every day for your kindness," she said, touching his face gently, not moving her hand and staring deeply into his eyes.

He laughed.

"Are you trying to hypnotize me?"

"No. I was just remembering how much you remind me of your dear brother, your mother, and your father."

Eager to switch gears, Christophe replied.

"Is the cemetery still in good shape since Uncle's stroke?"

"Sad to say, it needs work, but I am not up to it. As a matter of fact, Matthias took care of it before his death. He is buried there," she said sadly, recalling her husband.

Christophe stood and encircled her shoulder with his arm.

"I am so sorry I was unable to attend his services," he said.

"That's okay. Catrin and Margot came and they represented you well," she responded, sniffling. They were interrupted by the giggling of the girls in the yard.

"Look! Look, Pappa!" shouted Margot, her arms overflowing

with a wooly lamb that bleated feebly when the other girls caressed its head.

Christophe rubbed the lamb's head gently, and tried to dismiss the vision of grilled lamb chops with cilantro mint vinaigrette in his mind and the exquisite taste from his mouth.

"Do you still have draft horses?" he asked.

"No. Uncle Guillaume sold them and bought a tractor," said Jolien, as Guillaume experienced a rare flash of clarity.

"Roos, and Fleur!" he shouted, and laughed fondly in remembrance of the two giants.

Christophe remembered many nearly forgotten instances, and he longed for the simple life, wishing for a moment that he'd never strayed so far from home.

The girls chatted gaily as the cart, pulled by the well-used Ford N-Series tractor, bumped through the fields, scattering some sheep, swerving to avoid others that were too stupid to get out of the way. Christophe was the driver, and he knew the way to their objective which ended up in the forest. He was discouraged to see that the cemetery, without the loving care of Guillaume, had fallen into sad disrepair. Some of the older stones were leaning, others were grown over with lichen and moss, the grass was nearly knee high, and there were some virulent-looking vines snaking up the trunks of the trees on the perimeter. As Christophe and the girls unloaded the equipment off the cart, he reminded them to stay away from the vines, fearing that they were of the poison variety. He and Margot first tended the graves of Sander, Adelheide, and Armandus, while Justine and Manon started with the grave of their grandfather, Matthias.

"Did my grandparents and Armandus get along well with Mother?" said Margot, wielding a trowel, digging a shallow trench as she outlined a grave.

"Unfortunately, they never met her. I went away to school, the war came along, and I joined the Resistance. That's where I met

Catrin. By the time the war was over, my father, mother, and brother had been killed," he said, pausing from his labor to remember those awful times before continuing.

"I'm sure that you've heard the stories of their deaths; each one was attributed to friendly fire, with my mother dying of a broken heart."

"That must have been very difficult for you to take, Pappa," she said, dropping her trowel and hugging him.

"I was devastated. I hated the Allies for what they had done. But your mother played a major role in my healing."

"What did she do?"

"She told me to forgive them," he said as he returned to his work. He said a silent prayer that she would practice what she preached.

Christophe was sunburned, pleasantly sore from the manual labor, and itchy from the poison sumac that sought him out from the tree trunks. Other than those maladies, the visit had been a perfect respite from his worries and busy lifestyle—for a while anyway. The women and girls were chatting and laughing in the kitchen as they fixed supper, and he was in charge of Uncle Guillaume as they sat on the porch. Uncle Guillaume was in rare form this evening; one might say, "even bright."

"You remember Roos and Fleur?" he said, out of the blue.

"Yes, they were fine animals," said Christophe, as a jay squawked from the forest.

"That's a jay," said Guillaume, as if he were remembering an old friend. He spoke again.

"Do you remember Roos and Fleur?"

"Yes I do, quite well," said Christophe—patiently, lovingly.

"Do you remember when Roos stepped on your foot?"

"Actually, she stepped on Armandus' foot," chuckled Christophe.

The old man seemed confused and was silent for a while.

"Armandus came to see me last night," he said quietly, to Christophe's astonishment.

Curious, Christophe played the game.

"Really? What did he have to say?"

"He said that he missed you and was looking after your lady friend in China."

Deeply intrigued, Christophe didn't bother to correct him.

"How…how is she?"

"He said she is sad and wants to come home to you, but has lost her way."

Christophe was aggravated when they were interrupted by Margot.

"Aunt Jolien says it's time for you to come and eat," she said, and returned quickly to the kitchen to set the table.

Uncle Guillaume was mute, lost in whatever fragmented thoughts remained in his head.

Christophe stood and gripped the handles of the wheelchair.

"Let's go to supper, Uncle," he said, wishing that their conversation could have continued.

Guillaume reached over his shoulder and patted Christophe's hand with his icy fingers.

"Christophe? Please don't lose your way," he whispered as they entered the house.

The next day, as Christophe prepared for his journey home, he and Margot spoke lovingly to one another.

"I will miss you Pappa. And I miss Mamma terribly," said Margot, burying her head in Christophe's shoulder.

"I miss her too. She is in a dangerous situation, and if anything ever happened to her, I would die; I believe she went there to get away from me," he said, feeling ashamed for placing his burden of guilt on the shoulders of his twelve-year-old daughter.

"I believe she went there to find herself," said Margot.

"Perhaps. I promise you, Margot, when she returns I will do everything in my power to gain her forgiveness and guarantee that we can live as a family," he said, squeezing her shoulders tightly.

"Forgiveness, for what?" said Margot, pretending not to know of his philandering.

"I will tell you when the time is right. Promise me you will be careful this summer and keep in touch with me. Do you have your mother's address?"

"Yes. I started another letter to her before we left."

"Good. Please don't mention the conversation we've had today, okay?"

"Yes. I understand," said Margot, pitying her father and mother for the indiscretions that had ruined their marriage.

As Christophe drove down the road, he pondered Margot's wise words. He sincerely hoped that Catrin would find what she was looking for, and that he was part of the equation. He also vowed in his heart to his uncle that he would not lose his way in his resolve to make things right.

When he arrived home in Antwerp, he was eager to shower, stretch, and relax after the road trip. He had just settled down to open his mail when the phone rang.

Chapter 26

HOMECOMING

Emotionally and physically spent, Catrin was in pitiable shape when her commercial flight from London landed at Schiphol Airport in Amsterdam. She could have flown from London to Antwerp/Deurne airport, or rented a car at Schiphol for the trip home, which was only about 133 km away, but decided to stay at her property in Holland for a while to recuperate. Margot was spending the summer with relatives in the Ardennes and was unaware that her mother had returned, and Catrin had not bothered to contact Christophe of her arrival. She was more than eager to see them; however, she had a commitment to keep. Instead of proceeding directly to baggage claim, she booked a flight out of Schiphol to the United States, departure scheduled for a week from that day.

On arrival to her destination, she quickly unpacked, and after calling repeatedly, got in contact with Christophe.

"Catrin? You are home? Missionaries of the Sacred Heart informed me of what happened over there. They said that you were okay; I've been trying to get in touch with you; I was going to come to you, whether you wanted me to or not," he said frantically. He was surprised at her tone.

"Dear Christophe, I am sorry to have worried you. Does Margot know about this?"

"No, thank goodness, she is blissfully unaware, romping in the Ardennes with her cousins."

"Please don't tell her I'm home."

"I won't but may I come and see you?"

"I would love that, but I am ashamed of the way I look now...I would rather get some rest and be presentable for you and Margot. I am at the loft for a few days, then I have one more trip before I come home for good in Antwerp."

Christophe was disappointed that she would be leaving again, but thrilled at her kind responses to him as she continued.

"I would appreciate it if you and Margot would meet me at Antwerp's airport," she said, giving him the flight number, date, and time of her arrival.

"I'll be there, I promise," he said.

A week passed, and Catrin basked in the healing, calm refuge of the loft, which was situated on a quiet canal near the fishing village of Volendam. She spent a large part of her days sleeping, eating a wide variety of food and drink which she had been denied in her African journey-turned-nightmare. She enjoyed fresh air, sunny, cool days, and cooler nights that she hadn't realized she'd missed so much. Refreshed, she looked forward to the next part of her journey with heady anticipation.

The plane, bound for New York, took off on time, as they often did in those days. When the "fasten your seatbelt sign" was darkened, Catrin slid her carry-on bag from beneath the seat in front of her. She unzipped it, and for the second time that day, she inventoried items that she wouldn't dare ship with her luggage in the belly of the plane.

Had it not been for the concern and tender care of Julie, Bernard would have folded in on himself at the news of Bowman's horrific death. For some time afterward, he lay awake most of the nights, and during the daytime, went about his business in a catatonic state that most people thought was scary—a prelude to madness.

"Bernard, you're gonna have to start eatin' more, you're wastin' away to nothin'," said Julie, as they dressed to attend the memorial for Bowman at the university.

"I ain't that hungry," he said as Julie straightened his tie—a tie that once belonged to his brother. Bernard wished that he would actually waste away to nothing, and be relieved of the sadness and the guilt he felt for the loss of Bowman, who would never forgive him for killing the ones for whom he lived.

Bernard felt conspicuous as he and Julie were seated, along with the few family members surviving Bowman, in the front row of the auditorium. He squirmed uncomfortably in his borrowed suit as university staff members, and Bowman and Rosalee's pastor, praised Bowman for his goodness and contributions to the betterment of the human condition. Finally, Dr. Benton presented an eloquent eulogy. Afterwards, a long line of mourners filed by Bernard and Julie, extending their condolences. Last in the seemingly endless procession was Dr. Benton.

"Bernard, I can't imagine what you are feeling. I just want you to know that my family and I will always be here for you, and I would like for you to do me a favor."

Bernard was unable to reply, and Julie answered for him.

"Whatever you want, Dr. Benton."

Dr. Benton explained about the phone call he'd gotten from the Netherlands, and the appeal he'd received from the caller.

"Will you help me? It could be a good thing for you too," said Dr. Benton.

After a moment, Bernard nodded his head affirmatively. It was the least he could do for his brother.

It had been an exhausting day for Robert Benton. After the ceremonies were over, he sent his family home with promises to join them after he'd attended to some work in his office. He closed the blinds and sat down at his desk, surmising that his blood pressure was soaring as the hum in his ears moaned with a sorrowful undertone. Then he realized that the din was a replay of all that had been said and felt during the melancholy occasion, the choir of mourning voices led by his own deep baritone, which was laced with a monotone of sadness and guilt. Then he realized that the quiet of his inner sanctum heightened the clamor of anxiety that had been buzzing in his head all day. When he'd first heard of Bowman's demise, he was stunned, and immediately burdened with a sense of guilt for sending him to the Dark Continent to meet his end. He reached in his desk drawer, extracted a flask filled with Jim Beam, and took a heavy swallow. After experiencing a coughing fit, he spoke aloud amidst the buzzing and alternating silence.

"Bowman. I'm sorry. I hope you are at peace now."

The buzzing ceased, and Robert Benton sighed heavily, knowing that he had been forgiven. He laid his head on his desk and cried in relief.

As the plane lost altitude in preparation for landing in Knoxville, Catrin marveled at the majestic panorama below her: the substantial forests of the Ridge and Valley Appalachians, the tops of the trees reminding her of mounds of broccoli; the broad river valleys; the lakes, many of which were formed during the creation of the Tennessee Valley Authority; the lavender ridges and purple peaks of the grandiose Smoky Mountains in the distance. In no way did it bear any resemblance to the low, flat country of her native land or the arid plains of Africa.

"Ladies and gentlemen, in preparation for landing, please stow your personal belongings beneath your seats, lock your tray tables in position, as we are welcomed to McGhee Tyson Airport of Greater Knoxville. Thank you for flying United," came the flight attendant's voice over the tinny intercom. Catrin took one more look inside her carry-on bag before stuffing it beneath the seat again.

Julie drove. Bernard was quaking in anticipation of meeting Doctor de Jonge and didn't trust himself behind the wheel of their car, which he'd scrubbed and polished to a glossy sheen the day before.

"You think her plane will be on time?" he said, checking his fingernails for grease.

"You never know. I don't know much about airports," said Julie as she hastily turned right, almost missing the airport entrance.

"I've never been on a plane, and the only time I've ever been to an airport was when I dropped Bowman off at the terminal. He wouldn't let me come in…barely said good-bye," said Bernard sadly.

Julie found a parking spot on the third level of the garage. She and Bernard sat for a moment, frightfully excited.

"Well, let's do it," he said, as if he were going into battle.

Catrin was thankful that she spoke English; naturally, it made travel less chaotic in the States. Since her stay was not scheduled for a lengthy time, her luggage was minimal, and being trilingual reduced her time through customs in New York immeasurably. Now as she began embarkation from the plane, she smiled as the soft accents of southerners hung sweetly in the air and melted in her ears—reminding her of the long-ago downed flier from South Carolina, and of course, her beloved Bowman.

She smiled too, and was reminded that many cultures are the same when southerners hugged relatives and friends without reservation as they were greeted; joyous scenes that perhaps would have been played out a little more conservatively in her part of the world in Western Europe, but joyous just the same. She scanned the crowd of noisy celebrants, searching for her hosts, and found them standing shyly by a concrete pillar on the fringe of the crowd. They were just as Dr. Benton described them: the woman tall and thin, with dark hair swept back in a ponytail; the man tall and broad shouldered, with similar features to Bowman but rougher around the edges. He was holding a cardboard sign that was emblazoned with letters carefully drawn with a magic marker: *Doctor D.*

She approached them slowly.

"I am Catrin de Jonge, and I am guessing that you are Julie and Bernard. Am I not correct?"

Julie rushed to her, with Bernard trailing a few tentative steps behind.

"We sure are! Welcome to Tennessee, Doctor Deejong," said Julie, hugging Catrin warmly.

"We weren't sure how to spell your name, so we just wrote 'Dr. D.,'" said Bernard. He spoke shyly without eye contact as he handed her a small bouquet of flowers. She perceived that he said something about "flares."

She accepted them gracefully, with a little bow, realizing that the English word "flowers" was pronounced a little differently in this part of the world.

"That's the state flower of Tennessee, and we picked them out of Bowman's garden," said Julie proudly, as Catrin started to reach for her suitcase that floated in the sea of luggage on the carrousel.

"I'll get that," shouted Bernard, eager to make himself useful.

"And I'll carry your other bag," said Julie.

"Thank you. Would it be an imposition if I asked you to take me to my hotel?"

Julie laughed, but Bernard held a serious expression.

"If that means 'do we mind?' well, hell yes we mind. We have a room waiting for you at Bowman's house. And we've planned on showin' you around from there," she said.

"That is, if it's okay with you," said Bernard, touching her shoulder gently, like a shy child asking for a favor.

"That would be fine, but give me a moment to call and cancel my reservation," said Catrin, as she headed for the information desk. As she punched in the number on the phone, she thought that it was sweet and considerate that the couple referred to their home as "Bowman's house" rather than "the house."

The ride from the airport to Claiborne County was long: about two hours. Bernard drove this time and he was silent as Julie and Catrin conversed, getting to know one another.

"How long do you plan to stay?" said Julie, as they took the exit at Caryville off the main highway.

"My flight leaves from Knoxville the day after tomorrow," answered Catrin, marveling at the little lake alongside of the road, and the spine of lush, green mountains that seemed to stretch northward along the left side of the road forever.

"Actually, I didn't realize that it would take so long to arrive at your…Bowman's home. My plane leaves early on Friday morning, I must return soon, to my work and to take care of many details, and I think it would be prudent to spend the night at the Hilton near the airport. Would you mind taking me back tomorrow night? I am sorry, but I don't want to miss my flight," she apologized.

"Man, flying all the way here for just a day?" said Bernard.

"Hey. She's been through a lot and I'm sure she needs to get back to her family. We're honored that you came to see us, even though you can't do a lot of sightseein', aren't we, Bernard?"

"Sure," he said, eager to be relieved of unfamiliar company.

Catrin held back on explaining that the purpose of her visit wasn't to see the sights.

They slowed down to avoid speed traps as they travelled through the quiet little towns of Jacksboro and LaFollette.

"What kind of doctor are you, Catherine?" asked Bernard.

"It's pronounced *Cat-trin*," she laughed, "but you can call me Catherine if it's easier. Anyway, I am an epidemiologist—a person who tries to eradicate diseases," she said.

"Hell, I can't pronounce that either. I'll just tell folks that you're a doctor and you can tell them the rest, if that's okay," he laughed, and they all relaxed a bit more as the big valley opened up to them.

As Bernard let his guard down, he reminded Catrin more and more of Bowman—even charming, in a subtle way.

He pointed to a cluster of buildings on a hillside, the images seeming toylike with the big mountain looming over it.

"That there is Lincoln Memorial University. That's where Bowman was a perfessor," he said proudly.

"Oh yes, Dr. Benton," Catrin said, remembering the man who'd orchestrated this meeting.

Julie pointed northward beyond the university, and then, eastward.

"That's Cumberland Gap, up there, and yonder is Kentucky. Over there is Virginia. We're just a hop, skip, and a jump from all of them," she said.

Bernard turned on a gravel road that ran in a mostly straight line toward the mountains. To Catrin, the geography gradually appeared more like a tame version of Christophe's family's home in the Ardennes, with many trees, and a few homes and farms dotting the hillsides and scarce flat places. Finally, they turned on to a lane, identified with a sentinel mailbox with the name "Rafferty" painted on the side.

Julie clapped her hands together excitedly.

"OK, you can have your choice of any room in the house. This here was Bowman's room…"

"I'll take this," said Catrin, welcoming the opportunity to be close to the man.

"Where do you sleep?" she asked as Bernard placed her meager luggage on the bed.

"Oh, we live in town, at Bernard's apartment. But we're stayin' here while you're visitin'; you know, so you won't be scared of the dark," said Julie, not taking into consideration that Catrin had survived the evilest dark and the powers that inhabited that blackness on her own.

"Thank you, dear, I appreciate your company," said Catrin, wondering aloud why the couple did not live in the home.

"Oh, Bernard's apartment is close to his and my work. But I come up once a week to dust and clean, and Bernard works the crops on the weekends and when his work's slow, sometimes I help," said Julie, who changed the subject quickly.

"Alright. Just do what you want to do. Take a nap, walk around the farm; the bathroom's right down the hallway; Bernard just installed a new shower."

Catrin smiled at the word "share" as Julie continued.

"I'm gonna start cookin' some supper, and we'll get more caught up later, okay?"

"That sounds great to me. I think I will try out that new shower and take a power nap," said Catrin, as she partially unpacked her suitcase.

The shower did relax Catrin, but she was too wired to sleep. Nice smells floated from the kitchen and she followed them there. Julie took leave from her frying pan and welcomed her with a big hug.

"Well look what the cat drug in; hidey, Doctor," she said.

Catrin wasn't familiar with "the cat drug in" phrase but she wasn't offended, knowing that this sweet woman would never say anything offensive intentionally.

"I couldn't sleep; too wired, I guess, what are you cooking? It smells good."

"Fried chicken, taters, and beans, 'maters, onions, and cucumbers in vinegar," said Julie, as the chicken popped in the Lodge cast-iron skillet as a reminder of things to come.

"Let me put a lid on this and let's sit down at the table and talk."

As Catrin followed her suggestion, she struggled to translate "taters" and "'maters."

They were having a fine discussion when Bernard came in to the room with a beer in his hand. He seemed surprised to see Catrin, and self-conscious about the beer, setting it quickly on the counter.

"Doctor Catrin, I thought you would be asleep," he said apologetically.

"I was unable to sleep. Perhaps I could if you'd share one of those beers with me," she laughed.

He grinned. "All I've got is Bud, and it's in the refrigerator in the barn."

"Ah, that is kind of a Pilsner, isn't it? I'll have one, maybe two," she requested.

"Hell, bring a bunch, I got a wicked thirst goin', always happens when I fry chicken," said Julie, as he was out the door.

As the long night wore on, the three of them shared many

Budweisers and stories about their family, mostly Margot and Bowman. They became fast friends, and even confidants.

The beer loosened Bernard's reserve, and he summoned up great courage to ask the question.

"Did Bowman tell you about Rosalee and Durand?" he asked, his face showing his angst. Julie stared at him with wide-eyed astonishment.

"You mean when and how they died?" said Catrin, touching his arm tenderly.

"I swear to God, I didn't have nothin' to drink that night!" he said, covering his eyes with the heels of his hands.

"Bernard, it's okay, honey," said Julie, standing and holding his head in her hands.

"There's somethin' I've never told nobody, not even you, Julie, that I'd like to say tonight. Can I?" he pleaded. Julie sat down hard.

"Go on, baby, if it will make you feel better," she said, and Catrin nodded her head as he proceeded with the story.

"It was so foggy and rainy, we could hardly see. As we got near the top of the mountain, Durand asked if we could go in Cudjo's Cave. Rosalee told him it was closed. And I told him I heard there was haints of slaves and Civil War soldiers in there. He got real excited, and asked me to tell him about it. As he leaned forward, he spilled his soda pop down my neck. Rosalee screamed 'no' and I swerved the car into the other lane."

Bernard ceased telling the story briefly, as he tried to regain his composure. When he was able to continue, the women cried softly as he relived that horrific night—scene by scene, word by word.

"She didn't know what or if anything had happened to her little boy, and she didn't want him to live his life thinkin' that he was partly responsible for anything so bad," said Bernard in a barely heard voice. Julie scooted her chair over next to him and Catrin dabbed at her eyes with a paper napkin.

"As she was dyin' she begged me not to tell. I promised her; I would have promised that sweet woman anything; she was like a sister to me." His quiet sobs were the only sounds heard as a stunned silence enveloped the room.

"You've kept that secret all these years? It's been killin' you!" said Julie, running her hands through his thinning hair.

"I've wanted to die. But what I have mostly wanted was Bowman's forgiveness," he said, choking on his words, burying his head in his crossed forearms.

Catrin scooted her chair back abruptly.

"I'll be back in a moment."

"You ain't mad, are you?" said Bernard as he raised his head from the pillow of his arms.

"No. I am not angry. I've been looking for this opportunity for some time now," she said as she left the kitchen.

Julie formed the word "opportunity?" silently with her lips as she stared at her baffled man.

Catrin, in her eagerness, brought the entire bag back to the kitchen with her.

She sat at the table and unzipped it, all the while staring hard into Bernard's red-rimmed eyes.

"I want you to know that Bowman did forgive you, and in the last days of his life, he punished himself for never telling you. If he would have known about the full details of the accident, I am sure that he would have told you sooner."

"But I promised Rosalee," said Bernard as Julie comforted him.

"I know. And we honor you, and I am sure that Rosalee honors you for carrying out her request," she said, reaching into the bag.

"I believe Bowman had a premonition of his death and he asked me to give you one of his most cherished possessions that really speaks to how he felt... how he feels about you, his only brother," she said as she pulled the framed cross-stitched scene from the bag.

"I remember that. Rosalee made it for him and it hung in their bedroom," said Bernard.

"What are those words?" said Julie.

"They were put there by Rosalee to remind her man that forgiveness is what we owe ourselves for being human beings. He wanted me to give it to you, Bernard."

"What...what do the words mean?" said Bernard.

"They are French; they mean 'You are forgiven,'" she said in a whisper, as she placed the frame gently in his hands.

Bernard drew the frame to his chest and wailed long and hard. Julie and Catrin hugged one another as the burden of Bernard's torment was carried away on the notes of the primordial howl.

The next day, Bernard appeared as if he hadn't slept in a month. Actually, he had slept very well—better than he could remember. His drowsy appearance was really a reflection of his release from the anguish that had plagued him for so long.

"Bernard, I swear, you look like you're high on somethin'. You'd better let me drive; if the cops pulled you over, they'd throw you in jail," said Julie, as he loaded Catrin's bags in the car for the trip to the hotel.

"I think she's right," said Catrin. "You should ride in the rifle seat."

"That's 'shotgun,'" laughed Julie as she started the car.

They waited in the lobby as Catrin signed in at the desk of the hotel, which was located directly down the road from the airport

She approached them with a satisfied smile on her face.

"This is wonderful. I'm only a few steps from the airport," said Catrin.

"I hate to see you go so soon, but as early as you're leaving tomorrow, we would have had to leave Bowman's house at one o'clock in the morning," said Julie.

"I think it would be more appropriate to call it 'your house,'" said Catrin, as she hugged them both warmly.

"I'm really sorry that your stay was so short," said Bernard.

"I think my mission is accomplished, don't you?"

"I can't thank you enough, Catrin," said Bernard, as he took her hand and awkwardly held it to his cheek.

"I'll never forget the two of you, and Bowman Rafferty. He gave me reason to know that my life is important to others, especially the ones whom I've ignored, intentionally or not. Now go, before it gets dark. Au revoir," she said, kissing them both on the cheek. Bernard and Julie walked away, not daring to turn around for fear of crying.

The sun was on the verge of setting when they arrived at the house.

"Let's take a walk," said Bernard, and Julie was pleased because he wasn't normally one for taking walks.

"Where to?"

"Just up the hill to the graveyard."

Down in the hollows, it was becoming dark, but on the hilltop, the Rafferty family cemetery was lit gold and green by the waning sun. Bernard quickly found the resting places of Rosalee and Durand beneath the sour cherry tree, and knelt on one knee before them.

"Do you want me to leave you alone?" said Julie, moved by his reverence.

"No. Please stay," he said. And he spoke aloud in humble tones.

"Rosalee, Durand, I told. But I guess you already know that. I know that you forgive me, just like Bowman did. I love you all and I'll see you again someday," he said, and bent to touch their headstones respectfully after he stood up.

"Let's get back to our house, girl," he said.

EPILOGUE

As the days passed, Dikembe and Narolie had a difficult time keeping their newfound wealth a secret. It's a hard thing to do when you suddenly emerge from abject poverty into a life fulfilled with the necessities you've been denied for generations. Neighbors commented on the children's and Narolie's new clothing, new gardening tools and kitchen utensils, a secondhand radio, and relatively new furniture for the shade room. It was also noticed that when they visited a branch of the Bank du Congo, they were treated with respect rather than the contempt normally reserved for the desperately poor who rarely frequented the establishments. They made a generous, anonymous contribution to the clinic, and ordered tombstones made for the graves of many of those buried in the cemetery.

As the children splashed happily in the river below the bluff, Dikembe and Narolie puttered around the gravesites like gardeners—pruning, cutting away nature's debris which quickly takes over in a tropical climate, reclaiming the land, and sometimes its occupants. The pair was happy to take a break and rest in the shade of the Fountain tree nearby. The branches, filled with African tulips, swayed mesmerizingly in the breeze on the bluff; and the leaves shimmied and shook, responding to the caress of the air stream like dancers writhing seductively to the rumba beat of soukous artists reveling in muziki na biso ("our music") that wafted from the village below.

"The wind always seems high up here—much breezier than at our home down below," said Narolie, closing her eyes and lifting her face to enjoy the zephyr.

"Maybe it is a gift to the dead," said Dikembe as he rose to go, offering his hand to Narolie. The children's laughter mingled with the concert in the trees, and someone from below joined the orchestra as they played the Mbira, the thumb piano, and sang a familiar song.

"What is that song? I know it; I've known it all my life, but I can't think of the name," said Narolie, her apron fluttering, dancing in the wind as they walked.

Dikembe grinned, remembering one of his talks with Bowman.

"Lutuku y Bene Kanyoka—coming out of grief," he said as they neared Bowman's cross, the grave awaiting the tombstone they'd commissioned, but adorned now with the weighty sentiment scribbled in Lingala on a sheet of cardboard attached to the cross with wire:

Ndeko Bowman, who is now happy in the company of the stars.

"We feel your happiness, brother, because we are made of you," said Dikembe as they turned to depart.

Catrin was more anxious and excited on the last leg of her journey than she was about meeting Julie and Bernard. Bestowing the healing gift of the cross-stitch work on Bowman's behalf brought great joy; that experience, in her mind, would be a hard act to follow. But she would do her best to make the upcoming experience worthwhile, hopefully with the cooperation of all involved. Her heart beat wildly with anticipation as the jet followed the coastline of the North Sea into Antwerp.

The counterwoman at the flower shop was taken with the handsome man with the graying temples.

"What kind of bouquet would you like, sir?"

"Tulips; white tulips, preferably. 'Schoonoord.' Do you have them?"

"I'm sure we do. Let me look," she replied as she turned to enter the cooler.

"No problem," he answered, glancing at his watch, emphasizing that he was in a hurry.

The shopkeeper returned quickly with a beautiful bouquet of white tulips. He was so happy that he gave her a monstrous tip.

"White tulips are used to claim worthiness or send a message of forgiveness," she said, but her message was unheard as he raced out the door.

Traffic came to a halt not long after he returned to the highway. Soon, ambulance sirens were heard announcing the accident ahead. His anxiety at being late was tempered as he remembered the night he first presented her with the tulip bouquet. He could feel her soft lips on his as she whispered, "Je t'adore." And he was saddened to think that he might never hear those words, or feel that great love again, from anyone.

Catrin was disappointed that no one was there to greet her as she got off the plane. She hurried to baggage claim, hoping to find them there. But there was no one that she recognized. She glanced nervously around, wringing her hands as the conveyor belt spit luggage onto the revolving carrousel.

She paid little attention to finding her luggage, and hers was the only luggage remaining as it circled forlornly on the merry-go-round.

"Is that your luggage, madame?" said a burly skycap.

"Yes, yes it is," she said in a fog of worry and dismay.

"Would you like for me to take this to transportation?" he asked, pointing to his dolly. And he was interrupted.

"I'll take you home if you will allow me," said a male voice.

When they were settled in his car, he presented her with the bouquet of tulips. She smiled tenderly as the words "Je t'adore" rang, sweet as tiny bells, in her heart and mind.

"Margot and her cousins are on a beach trip to Rotterdam, but I will pick her up this weekend. You are welcome to go along if you'd like," he said. But she was heedless of his remarks in her eagerness to make known her epiphany.

"Christophe, I have so much to tell you, I hope you have time to listen. I assure you that what I have to say will be astonishing," she said.

"I have plenty of time. Please forgive me for being late today," he said.

"Tu es pardonné...for everything," she replied, echoing the holy words of just and pious men, and angels, like Armandus Peeters and Bowman Rafferty.

As they drove home, they talked—mostly about the blessings in their lives. They rode in silence for a while, reveling in the heady fragrance of the bouquet, and the prospects of life to come.

CPSIA information can be obtained at www.ICGtesting.com
Printed in the USA
LVOW11s0239190915

454827LV00001B/72/P